Fables and Legends of Ireland

Fables and Legends of Ireland

Maureen Donegan

MERCIER PRESS
Douglas Village, Cork, Ireland
www.mercierpress.ie

Trade enquiries to Columba Mercier Distribution,
55a Spruce Avenue, Stillorgan Industrial Park, Blackrock, Dublin

This Edition 2004

ISBN 185635 441 5

10 9 8 7 6 5 4 3 2 1

FOR MY FAMILY

Printed in Ireland by ColourBooks Ltd

Contents

Preface

This is not a scholarly book – I see learned heads nodding in agreement – but it is an attempt to bring the lovely old stories of heroic Ireland to a wider audience than that of the schoolroom, or of the Irish scholar.

These tales were told and retold by word of mouth and, although they are full of magical creatures and enchanted castles, they are also about people: real people who suffered from indigestion and jealousy, just as we do.

I first came across the Táin Bó while doing research for quite a different kind of book; I dipped into Cecile O'Rahilly's excellent translation from the *Book of Leinster* and was unable to put it down. Maeve and Ailill and Fergus and Cúchulainn are as alive today as they were when their history was finally captured in the yellow pages of eleventh- and twelfth-century manuscripts; the polished sarcasm of the royal pair is reflected in many a modern marriage, and Cúchulainn's vanity and the divided loyalties of Fergus are as old and as new as time.

These sagas and myths are part of a much larger stream of literature which extended from Iceland across Europe. In 'The Voyage of Maildún' one is irresistibly reminded of Jason in search of the Golden Fleece but, although Maildún's adventures are as bizarre and fantastic as one could imagine, throughout he remains endearingly human; pig-headed almost to the last and all too easily led astray by a pretty face. Indeed all the heroes – and anti-heroes – of the tales suffered from the same susceptibility. They could no more sense a scheming witch behind blue eyes and a fair face than they could avoid the bloody wars into which their pride and avarice, and sometimes their compassion, led them.

The Fianna, though, larger than life and swashbuckling across Ireland even into fairy cities beyond the sea, remain my favourites. Even Conan Maol with his tactless tongue and his incessant grumbling inspires a kind of reluctant affection and the little episode of 'The Magic Cloak', which was first recorded in verse in the *Book of the Dun Cow*, is a perfect and timeless picture of the incessant wars between the sexes.

1

THE BIRTH OF THE BULLS

It's as difficult to say what the precise cause of the great cattle raid was as it is to pinpoint the start of any war. Nevertheless the main protagonists, the true enemies at the beginning and in the middle and at the end, were the powerful and magical bulls of Ireland: the Donn Cuailnge and the Finnbennach.

The Donn Cuailnge, the brown bull of Ulster, was enormous and brimming with rude health. He could bull fifty heifers every day and they calved in less than twenty-four hours or burst their sides with the effort. He was broad enough for fifty youths to play across his back and tall enough to shelter a hundred warriors beneath him. Narrow-flanked and broad-breasted, he was as brave as he was ferocious, and as crafty as he was strong, and he had a right royal rage. Even spectres and spirits kept away from his glen when he pawed the earth throwing black turf across his back and growling and glaring at all comers. But he was handsome too, with a proud, curling brown head and a strong thick neck. His cows adored him and, in the evening, when he came to his byre, he made a musical lowing so melodious and unforgettable that no one in all of Cuailnge ever wished for other music.

Only the Finnbennach came near to matching him in power and beauty. The Finnbennach ruled the animals of Connacht absolutely. Because of him no male animal dared utter a sound louder than the lowing of a cow. He had a white head and white feet, but his body was the red colour of blood and his breast was as strong as a stallion's. When he stood among the cows of Ailill and Maeve, bellowing his greatness to the world, he was indeed a hero to his herd. He would swish his tail, and kick up his great hooves, and lift his haughty snout to the sky, proclaiming his victory over all things. He was strong and proud and in his prime, and he had the aid of demons.

Needless to say, they were not ordinary creatures, nor did they start out as bulls. They began, simply enough, as two swineherds. Fruich was the name of one. His master was Bodb, the king of the fairy creatures of Munster, and Rucht was the name of the other. His king, Ochall, ruled the fairy kingdom of Connacht, and being both of magical people the two swineherds were able to change into any shape they pleased.

They met, predictably enough, in the course of their work. When there was a glut of acorns and beech nuts in Munster, Ochall would send his swineherd with his pigs to feed in the south and when, in other years, there was plenty of food in Connacht Bodb would send his swineherd north to fatten up his stock. And so the years went by amicably enough with a steady friendship ripening between Fruich and Rucht (Fruich was called after a boar's bristle and Rucht after its grunt).

However it wasn't long before the Connacht people began to boast that their herdsman was more powerful than his southern colleague but when the Munster people heard that they denied it vigorously, and said that of course their pig-keeper was much more powerful than Ochall's. The next year, when Ochall's swineherd came south he got a very cool reception.

'Is it you who is trying to cause trouble between us?' asked Bodb's swineherd. 'They say you are more powerful than me.'

'I'm certainly no less so,' Ochall's swineherd said.

'Then we'll test it,' Bodb's swineherd said. 'I'll cast a spell over your pigs so that whatever they eat they won't gain a scrap of weight.'

He cast the spell, and it worked. It worked so well that Ochall had to take his pigs back home at the end of the season as thin and as wretched as when he had come, and when he got home he was the laughing stock of Connacht.

'That proves nothing,' he said to himself, trying to ignore the jeering. 'I can cast a spell or two myself.'

He bided his time and, when hard times fell on Munster and Bodb's swineherd had to come north in search of food for his pigs, Ochall's swineherd played the same trick, and Bodb's swineherd had to go home with a lean and miserable herd of pigs to face the mockery of Munster.

The whole affair proved nothing except that they were equal, and before long they were even more equal because they were both dismissed from their jobs.

In disgust they took the shape of ravens and fought a long and loud battle in the sky above Connacht. They fought for a year with no result, and then they flew south and fought for another year over Munster. The noise was unbearable and the people of Munster gathered together on the plain and grumbled among themselves.

'It goes on and on,' they said, 'and we're tired of it.'

Just then a steward from Ochall's palace in Connacht came up the hill towards them.

'They're making as much din as the birds we had in Connacht

last year,' he said. 'You'd swear they were the same ones.'

And at this the two birds of prey turned back into human shapes and the people recognised the former swineherds and welcomed them home.

'We are welcome nowhere,' Bodb's pig-keeper said. 'We bring only sorrow and death and slaughter between friends.'

'I don't understand,' the king said, when they were brought before him. 'What have you been doing all this time?'

'Fighting,' his swineherd said, simply. 'We took the shape of ravens and fought for a year over Connacht, and for a year over Munster, and now we are going to take the shape of water creatures for two years and see what becomes of that.'

They parted, there on the hill, and hurried away. Each turned into a huge water beast; one headed for the Shannon and the other for the Suir.

They met first in the Suir and fought a great battle, biting and snapping at each other with enormous jaws, and then they carried their fight to the Shannon and the men of Connacht gathered on the river bank to watch them. Each fish had a head the size of the top of a mountain and the spray from their jaws reached up as far as the sky but, although it was a marvellous entertainment for the huge and ever-growing crowd led by King Ochall, neither was able to master the other.

Wearily the two water creatures declared a truce and climbed out of the river and on to the bank, and there they resumed the shape of men.

'Well?' Ochall said. He had been waiting at the river's edge.

His swineherd sighed. 'Nothing goes well,' he said. 'Two years' strife and no result. We are going to try as stags.'

He looked inquiringly at Bodb's swineherd who nodded, and then they parted again, each to his own part of the country.

For the next two years the people of Ireland were disturbed by the clashing of antlers and the scattering of herds of young deer, and for two years after that by two phantoms pursuing each other on the land and in the air, and terrifying both themselves and those who saw them. After that they were two dragons breathing fire and snow alternatively and with no consideration for who might be in the way.

They met again, in the seventh year, in the shape of men on neutral ground.

'Do you admit defeat?' asked Ochall's swineherd.

'Certainly not. Do you?' asked Bodb's.

'Then we will fight as men,' Ochall's swineherd said.

And fight they did and brought their two provinces into the bitter conflict with them. No one knew that the two mighty champions whose deeds outdid each other's in courage and strength were in fact the two former swineherds. Now Bodb's man was named Rinn, and Ochall's Faebur.

Finally there was a huge assembly by Loch Riach. The encampments were brilliant with rich garments and precious metals. Bodb brought seven times twenty horsemen and seven times twenty carts. Each man was of royal blood, and each matching dappled horse wore a silver bridle. The riders wore red-folded cloaks edged with spun gold, and green cloaks flung about their shoulders and fastened with a silver brooch. There was no end to the luxury of their trappings from their white and gold embossed shields to the heavy jewel-encrusted coronets on their heads. It is said that seven times twenty women and children died at the sight of them.

Perhaps it was their preoccupation with their appearance and the effect it had that made them over-confident. They marched arrogantly to meet Ochall, leaving their camp and carts and horses unguarded and, while Ochall kept them in conversation, the Connacht men quickly surrounded the Munster troop, gold coronets and silver shields notwithstanding. They literally squashed the Munster army; wherever a Connacht man sat a Munster man died beneath him.

'Welcome,' Ochall said to Bodb, surveying the carnage.

'Welcome?' Bodb said.

'I came only to talk,' said the king of the Munster fairies. 'With kings and queens,' he added, 'but I can't see many here.'

Ochall sighed. 'They have gone ...young people ...' he sighed again.

'Then we should protect each other,' Bodb said.

Ochall looked pointedly at the remains of the Munster army.

'Why should I need your protection?' he said.

'Look to the north,' Bodb said, and Ochall turned and saw a vast independent group of warriors approaching the assembly. They were resplendent in crimson and white with blue-black cloaks. They set up camp a little distance away and watched the proceedings quietly, fingering their bronze swords which they had hidden under their cloaks. Their sharp-edged white-bronzed shields they kept on their backs.

'And as well as that,' Bodb said, 'I have a champion to help you.' He brought forward Rinn.

'Those are Connacht men,' Ochall said, looking at the newcomers anxiously, 'and they will give me their allegiance.'

'But will they find you a champion to fight Rinn?' Bodb said.

Mainchenn, a druid from Britain, watched the proceedings with disgust. Pacts were made and older ones betrayed; independent men sold their birthright for royal favour; twenty northern men dropped dead with fright when they saw the mighty king of the Munster fairies, depleted though his army was, but still no one could be found to fight the southern champion, Rinn.

And then Faebur stepped forward. 'I will fight him,' he said, and Rinn, who until this time had watched all the would-be warriors with disdain, stepped back and said that Faebur's was not an acceptable challenge.

But Faebur was not going to be turned aside. He rushed at Rinn and the bloodiest fight of all took place. They lashed at each other for three days and three nights, striking so hard that their lungs could be seen, and then in the white heat of battle they released themselves once more from the human shape and became demons again, and scores of people died at the sight of them.

Bodb eventually claimed victory over the Connacht men. Even when the kings of Leinster and Meath came to Ochall's aid, Bodb was still victorious. The champions had resumed their earthly shape and were once again hacking each other to bits, but Bodb ordered the field to be cleared of slaughter and then he gathered up the two warriors and took them into his charge.

They next appeared in much more humble incarnations, that of two water worms. One of them went to Connacht, where Maeve had become queen, and the other went to Cuailnge in Ulster where he was eventually found by Daire Mac Fiachna.

Maeve was the first to accost her worm. She had gone to the well to wash her hands and face when she dipped her white-bronze container in the water and the little worm swam into it. He was every colour and hue of the spectrum and Maeve poured away the water so that she could have a better look at him.

'Truly,' she said, 'you are a very beautiful creature. What a pity you can't speak.'

'I can speak,' the worm said, and then Maeve knew it was indeed a magical creature.

'Why are you disguised as such a small animal?' she said.

'I am a very troubled animal,' he said. 'I have been many shapes but in this one I have managed to find a little peace.'

Maeve listened to him gravely. 'Things have been very difficult for you,' she said, 'but I wonder what the future holds for me now that I'm queen?'

'You should take a husband,' the worm said. 'You are rich ...' he paused and gave a little wriggle, 'and beautiful ...'

'Ah,' Maeve said, 'but if I take a Connacht man how do I know that he won't try to take over the kingdom?'

'I know exactly the man for you,' said the worm. 'Ailill the son of Ruad of Leinster. He is a fine young man without fault. He will not be jealous or try to take your place.'

'Mmm,' Maeve said, doubtfully. 'But is he ...?' She hesitated.

'His beauty and ardour and strength will match your own,' the worm said.

Maeve was pleased. 'And how can I help you?' she asked.

'Bring me food every day to the stream,' the worm said. He

gave another little wriggle. 'My name is Cruinnic,' he said.

Daire mac Fiachna came across his worm in much the same way. As he was washing his hands in a stream in Cuailnge a small multicoloured creature watched him gravely from a stone. Daire moved back hastily. He had never seen anything like it before and he was afraid.

'Don't run away,' said the worm, 'I have a lot of things to say to you.'

'What can we have to say to each other?' Daire asked nervously.

'First I have to tell you that you will find a ship full of treasure.'

Daire stopped being nervous. 'Treasure?' he said. 'And what else?'

'And after that,' the worm said, 'you will confer maintenance and goods on me.'

'What kinds of goods?'

'Food,' the worm said.

'Why should I give you food?' Daire asked.

'Because I'm starving,' the worm said, raising his voice.

'There is food in the stream,' Daire said.

'Not for me,' the worm said, 'I'm not a fish.'

'Then what –?'

'I'm Bodb's swineherd,' the worm said, drawing himself up to his full two inches. 'My name is Tuinniuc, and my colleague is over there in Connacht being fed off the fat of the land by Maeve and I'm getting weaker and weaker by the day …'

'Yes – I think I've heard of you,' Daire said, hastily.

'Then don't ask silly questions,' the worm said, 'and bring me some food.'

And so Daire undertook to feed the worm every day with his own hands for the period of one year, just as Maeve, in Connacht, was feeding Cruinnic.

The prophecies came true. Maeve married Ailill and Daire's treasure ship made him rich, and in their separate streams the worms grew fat and strong – and restless.

'I have something to tell you,' Tuinniuc said one day when Daire brought his customary meal.

'What is it?' Daire asked. 'Aren't things going well for us?'

'For you, maybe,' Tuinniuc said, 'you have corn and milk in abundance.'

'Haven't I looked after you?' Daire said.

'Yes,' the worm said. He sighed. 'But the battle – feud – I can feel it welling up inside me. I have to fight Ochall's swineherd once more.'

'How can you do that?' Daire asked. He paused, delicately. 'Situated as you are?'

'Tomorrow,' the worm said, 'one of your cows will drink me and, at the same moment in Connacht, Cruinnic will be drunk by one of Maeve's cows.'

'But how will that help?' Daire said.

'Then two calves will be born.'

'Calves?' Daire said.

'Bull calves,' the worm said. 'And a great battle will be fought.' He slid off the stone into the water. 'Goodbye,' he said, and disappeared.

And it happened exactly as Tuinniuc said. Cruinnic was swallowed by one of Maeve's cows at the stream near her palace, and simultaneously Tuinniuc disappeared down the throat of a thirsty Ulster cow. In the course of time two calves were born and they grew into the most beautiful and feared bulls in Ireland: the white bull Finnbennach in the west, and the brown bull, Donn Cuailnge in Ulster. Their horns were decorated with gold and silver and their roars were heard the length and breadth of the land. The Finnbennach was strong and fierce and cunning; the Donn Cuailnge was named for the ancient God of the Dead.

2

The Pillow Talk of Ailill and Maeve

Ailill settled himself in their royal bed in Connacht.

'Isn't it a fine thing,' he said, 'for a woman to be married to a nobleman?'

Maeve adjusted her pillow and smiled at him agreeably.

'What makes you think that?' she said.

'Because you were never so well off in your life.'

'That's not true,' Maeve said, still agreeable. 'I was well off before I met you.'

'At one time, perhaps,' Ailill said, 'but wealth is a relative thing.' He paused. 'How many times had you been robbed?'

'There was nothing wrong with our army,' Maeve said, sharply.

'No one can afford constant raids and losses. You know your lands were run down.'

'My father,' Maeve said, with an edge in her voice, 'was in the high-kingship of Ireland.'

'Yes,' Ailill said, 'but …'

'No buts. He was in the high-kingship of Ireland and he had six daughters, and of those six I was the most noble. I was the one who was the best endowed and bravest in battle. Do you know how many mercenaries I had from abroad?'

'Yes,' Ailill said. He sighed.

'Fifteen hundred,' Maeve said, 'and all royal. And another fifteen hundred from my own province. Do you know how many men each one had?'

'Yes,' Ailill said, but Maeve wasn't listening.

'Ten men,' she said, triumphantly, 'and nine men for each mercenary, and eight men for each mercenary and seven men for each mercenary …'

Ailill held up his hand and closed his eyes as she enumerated her limitless household.

'… and for that reason,' she said, 'my father gave me one of the Provinces of Ireland, Cruachú, and I was known as Maeve Cruachú. And still am,' she said, as an afterthought.

Ailill pulled the covers around his ears.

'All the kings of Ireland sought my hand in marriage, Maeve continued. She ticked them off on her fingers. 'The king of Leinster and the king of Tara and the king of Ulster …'

'Why did you turn them all down?' said Ailill.

'I wanted a special kind of a man,' Maeve said. Her voice softened. 'I wanted a man of courage who was neither mean nor jealous. I wanted such a man as no woman has ever asked for in the whole of Ireland.'

Ailill grunted.

'And you came highly recommended,' Maeve said, thinking of the worm who had spoken to her in the stream. 'I am generous and I couldn't live with a mean man. I give gifts freely and so do you.'

Ailill grunted again.

'And it wouldn't do if you were timid – which you are not – because I am brave in battle, even in single-handed combats, and we must be matched in courage.' She paused. 'And if you were jealous …'

'Yes?' Ailill said.

'… which you are not,' Maeve said, quickly, 'then we could not live together at all, because I never lack a lover.' She stroked Ailill's head. 'But you, Ailill, are such a man as I searched for. You are not penny-pinching, nor jealous, and you do not hang back in battle.'

Ailill opened his mouth to speak, but Maeve swept on.

'But if I am a fortunate woman, then you are a most fortunate man. You have a dowry such as only I, Maeve Cruachú, could give you: the raiment of twelve men; the finest chariot; the breadth of your face in red gold and the weight of your left arm in white bronze. No one can claim anything from you that I did not bring you because you are dependent on my marriage portion.'

'That is not so,' Ailill said. ' My brothers are kings but they are no wealthier than I am. I left them to their portion because I am the younger son, but I claimed this province by virtue of my mother's rights. This province,' he said, in a tone which did not brook any contradiction, 'was the only one in Ireland dependent on a woman.'

Maeve sat bolt upright in bed.

'And what better queen could I have,' Ailill said, hastily, 'than you who are the daughter of the high-king of Ireland?'

'My property is greater than yours,' Maeve said, flatly.

'I marvel,' Ailill said, 'that you can say such a thing. There is no one in Ireland who has more possessions and wealth than I have.'

Maeve pushed back the covers and clapped her hands.

'What are you doing now?' Ailill said, wearily.

'We will see who has the greater possessions,' Maeve said. 'We will see here and now.'

A servant came in to answer her summons and Maeve instructed her to bring in some of the least valuable of their possessions, so that they could make comparisons.

'You will see,' she said to Ailill, 'that even in small things my goods outshine yours.'

The servants brought in some wooden cups and vats, and iron vessels and Maeve and Ailill looked at them and could not find any difference.

'Bring something better,' Maeve said, 'our jewellery –'

Their rings were brought in and their bracelets and their thumb-rings, and their gold treasures.

'They are the same,' Ailill said. 'We are equal.'

'Bring my purple gown,' Maeve said, suddenly.

'And mine,' Ailill said. The servants brought them in and for each garment of Maeve's he had one to match, blue and black and green, yellow and multi-coloured and grey, brown and checked and striped.

Maeve got out of bed and crossed to the window.

'Bring in all the sheep,' she said, and the servants looked at her in surprise then ran to do her bidding. The sheep were driven in from the fields and open plains and assembled on the lawn below them. They were counted and compared and for each sheep of Ailill's was one of equal size in Maeve's flock. Among Maeve's flock there was a splendid ram and she showed it to Ailill triumphantly, but a ram was found among his flock which proved to be its equal.

'Bring the horses,' Maeve said, grimly, and they were brought in from the paddocks and grazing land. Maeve's horse-herd had a splendid horse of great value.

'This time,' she said, 'I have the better of you,' but Ailill had a horse to match him.

Then the great herds of swine were brought from the woods and remote bushland. They were counted and identified and although Maeve had a special boar, Ailill had another.

Ailill leaned back on his pillows and smiled.

'Do you want to compare our cattle?' he asked.

'Certainly!' Maeve said.

The cattle were brought in, in droves, from the woods and open plains of the entire province, and they were counted and found to be equal in number and in size and in quality. But among Ailill's cows there was a special bull. His name was Finnbennach.

'He is my bull,' Maeve said. 'He was calf to one of my cows.'

'He does not wish to belong to a woman,' Ailill said. There was feeling in his voice. 'He has taken his place in my herd.'

'Then I will have a bull to match him!' Maeve said, flinging herself across the room. 'One who recognises a powerful queen. A queen in her own right,' she added emphatically. 'Fetch Mac Roth the herald,' she shouted.

'It's only a bull,' Ailill said. 'We are almost equal.'

'I will not be inferior to you in this!' Maeve said, 'or in anything.'

Mac Roth came quickly in answer to her summons. The palace was buzzing with the queen's anger.

'Where,' Maeve demanded, 'is there a bull such as Finnbennach?'

'There is only one better in the whole of Ireland,' Mac Roth said. 'His name is Donn Cuailnge and he belongs to Daire mac

Fiachna of Ulster.'

'Daire mac Fiachna?' Maeve said. She thought for a while. 'I will have the loan of him for a year. Will you go, Mac Roth, and ask Daire for him. Tell him …' she hesitated. 'Tell him I will give him a fee of fifty heifers when I return the bull.'

Mac Roth looked doubtful.

'If his people don't want him to lend Donn Cuailnge,' Maeve said, sharply, 'let Daire come down himself with his bull and I will give him the equal of his own land in the plain.'

'Maeve!' Ailill said.

She ignored him. '… and a fine chariot such as I brought as a dowry to Ailill, and more than that …'

'Yes?' said Mac Roth.

'Tell him he shall have my most willing thighs.'

Mac Roth set out on his mission as soon as he had assembled nine messengers to go with him. He left behind him a pale and silent Ailill, and a very determined Maeve.

At first all went well. Mac Roth, as the most important of the emissaries, was welcomed with great courtesy by Daire himself in his private chamber.

'What brings you to Cuailnge, my friend?' Daire asked, and Mac Roth told him of the dispute between Maeve and Ailill.

'Queen Maeve requests the loan of Donn Cuailnge to match the Finnbennach,' he said. 'She will give you fifty heifers and return the bull to you at the end of the year.'

'Mmm,' Daire said.

'And if you come yourself,' Mac Roth said, as Daire hesitated, 'she will give you an area equal to your own lands in the level plain of Mag Ai, and a chariot such as she gave the king on their marriage.'

'Does she know that the Finnbennach is no match for Donn Cuailnge, that my bull is feared and respected through the length and breadth of Ireland?'

'She does,' Mac Roth said, 'and for that reason she has told me to tell you that if you loan her Donn Cuailnge she will give you her most willing thighs.'

'In that case,' Daire said, shaking himself with such enormous pleasure that the seams of his flock bed burst and scattered their contents over him, 'in that case nothing, not even the men of Ulster, will stop me from sending Donn Cuailnge to Maeve in Connacht.'

Mac Roth smiled and brushed flock off his tunic and said that he was even more pleased with the answer he had got.

'And Maeve will be pleased too,' he said.

Daire smiled. 'To celebrate you shall eat and drink of the best we have in Ulster.'

Mac Roth went back to his companions and they were attended by the servants of the house. Fresh rushes and straw were spread on the floor and the choicest food brought in. It was accompanied by enough wine and mead to loosen the most cautious tongue and soften the hardest head.

'Our host is very generous,' one of the messengers said to another.

'He is indeed.'

'The most generous in Ulster,' said the first, slurring the words slightly.

'He's not as powerful as Conchobor,' said the second. 'Daire is only his vassal.'

'But the Donn Cuailnge is a wonderful prize,' the first man said, 'and it takes a great man to give to us what it would have taken all the forces of the four provinces of Ireland to carry off from Ulster.'

The other man looked at him disbelievingly.

'Our host is a generous man,' the first man repeated.

'The most generous in Ulster,' another said, overhearing.

'No one more generous,' the first messenger said, banging his fist on the table.

'He is Conchobor's man, that's all,' the second man said again.

'But he gave us the bull,' the first man said, getting drunkenly to his feet, 'and we couldn't have taken it without his leave.'

'Who couldn't?' his companion said, pushing him. 'We would have taken it by force – easily – if he didn't give it to us.'

They all joined in the argument and the first messenger was put firmly in his place.

'All right,' one of them said. He had drunk slightly less than the others. 'Here we are sitting at Daire's table, eating his food and accepting his generosity but – I still think we could have marched in here and stolen the bull and he couldn't have stopped us.'

A babel of voices broke out and for a moment no one noticed Daire's butler coming quietly into the room with more food and drink. The butler stood and listened and then the messengers saw him and stopped talking. They looked at each other awkwardly, wondering if he had heard them. The butler told the servants to put down the trays of food, and then he hurried away without a word and went to report to Daire.

'Was it you,' he asked, 'who gave our prize, our very own Donn Cuailnge, to those messengers from Connacht?'

'It was,' Daire said. 'Why?'

'Because they are saying that if you didn't give him to them they would have taken him by force, that the armies of Maeve and Ailill with Fergus leading them would carry off any prize.'

It was Daire's turn to fly into a temper.

'I swear by all the gods!' he said, 'that they will have to take him by force or he stays here in Cuailnge. How dare they abuse my hospitality?'

They spent the rest of the night brooding over the ingratitude of Connacht men, the imprudence of giving fine wine to ignorant messengers, and the unbelievable gall of certain royal people, who should know better, thinking that they could take and plunder as they wished from strong Ulster soldiers.

The next morning an unsuspecting Mac Roth went with his companions to ask Daire where they might find Donn Cuailnge.

'Noble sir,' Mac Roth began, but Daire, furious, interrupted him.

'I'd have you all killed!' Daire shouted, 'if I wasn't a fair man. As it is ...'

Mac Roth looked bewildered. He also had a headache. 'What is it?' he said.

'You said if I didn't give you the bull willingly you and your armies would take him by force.' Daire was frothing at the mouth with temper. 'You said Ailill and Maeve's army with Fergus leading them would come to Ulster and take the Donn Cuailnge.'

'That was just the messengers boasting and jesting. They'd had a lot to drink,' Mac Roth said. 'They were …' his voice trailed off when he saw Daire's expression.

'You ate my food and you drank my wine, and then you insulted me,' Daire said. He turned away coldly. 'You will not take the bull.' He nodded to his servants. 'The visitors from Connacht are leaving,' he said.

Mac Roth saw that it was useless. He sighed and gathered up the messengers and told them the bad new, and they returned reluctantly and empty-handed to Cruachú. Maeve was waiting for them.

'Well,' she said, 'where is Donn Cuailnge?'

'We didn't bring him,' Mac Roth said.

'Why not?' Maeve demanded.

Mac Roth hesitantly began to tell her what had happened but before he could finish Maeve stopped frowning and the light of battle lit in her eye.

'It was an excuse,' she said. 'I can see that now. Of course they would not give the bull unless we took it by force.' She paused. 'And that is exactly what we will do.'

Straightaway messengers went out to all Maeve's followers and during the next few weeks thousands of warriors arrived at Cruachú to support her. They came marching in magnificent columns, some with shorn heads and green and silver cloaks, and others in grey and white with swords of gold and silver. The last band had flowing hair, bright yellow and god, streaming down their backs, and they wore purple embroidered cloaks flung around their shoulders and fastened with golden inset brooches. They marched together in perfect unison and Maeve watched them coming proudly.

'Such a sight,' she said to Ailill.

The armies camped together for a full fortnight in Connacht. The air was black from the smoke of their camp fires and they spent their time feasting and drinking and singing to take their minds from the coming conflict.

Maeve left them towards the end of their resting time and went in her chariot in search of her druid to ask him what was to befall them.

'They have left their families and their friends and their land,' Maeve said, 'and I will be blamed for those who do not return. They are all as dear to me as life itself but it is on me that their curses will fall.'

'You will come back,' the druid said, 'whoever falls it won't be you.'

Welcome as the news was, it was not precisely what Maeve wanted to hear. She went back to her chariot, thoughtfully, and then started as she caught sight of a girl coming towards her. She was weaving a fringe of red gold, holding the threads in her hand as she walked. The girl was dressed in a speckled green cloak with a round, heavy brooch holding it at her breast, and she was very beautiful. Every part of her was perfect from the coils of her golden head to the sharp pink tips of her long white feet. She had clear bright skin with laughing eyes and thin red lips enclosing shining pearly teeth and her sweet voice was like the music plucked from the strings of a harp by a master hand. Maeve could see the lustre of her white body shining through her garments and, behind her, one of her golden tresses falling to the calves of her legs.

'What are you doing here?' Maeve asked.

'Promoting your interests,' the girl said, 'and mustering all the provinces of Ireland to go with you to Ulster to carry off Donn Cuailnge.'

'And what business is that of yours?' Maeve asked.

'I am a bondmaid of your people,' the girl said, simply. 'That is my reason.'

'I don't know you,' Maeve said. 'Who are you?'

'I am Feidelm, the prophetess,' the girl said.

'A prophetess,' Maeve said, thoughtfully, 'and how do you see our army?'

'I see red. I see crimson,' Feidelm said.

'Conchobor is ill – I have sent my spies out – so we have nothing to fear from him. He will not fight,' Maeve said, sharply. 'How do you see our army now?'

'I see red. I see crimson.'

'And Mac Conchobuir is also laid low. I have sent my spies to every corner of Ulster,' Maeve glared at her. 'How do you see our armies now?'

'I see red upon them. I see crimson.'

'And Mac Durthacht has retired to Ráth Airthir. We have nothing to fear from Ulstermen. So tell me the truth, Feidelm, how do you see our army?'

Feidelm would not be moved. 'I see red on them. I see crimson.'

'Mac Cuthechair has locked himself in his fortress. I tell you we have nothing to fear. Tell the truth, prophetess, how do you see our army?'

'I see red,' Feidelm said, snapping together her narrow red lips, 'and I see crimson.'

'All right,' Maeve said, 'I'll give you this – when the men of Ireland get together there are always little difficulties as to who shall lead the van, or who will be first to cross the river, or first to kill a boar or stag or game, or even who shall bring up the rear, but these things are of no account …'

'I see red,' Feidelm chanted. 'I see crimson.'

Maeve made to get into her chariot and return to her armies but the girl called her back.

'I see a fair man who will perform great weapon feats. He wears a red mantle and a hero's light shines in his eyes.'

'I do not know this man,' Maeve said.

'He has the seven lights of a hero in his eyes, and his brow is as virtuous as it is fair.'

Maeve lifted her chin in a determined way.

'He is beloved of women,' Feidelm said, 'but in battle he is transformed into a savage dragon-shape, and your army will be blood-stained from him. He has four swords of great renown and each one has its special use …' Feidelm had got into her stride and was not to be stopped, 'and he carries his Gae-Bolga as well as his sword and spear. Two spears are tied to the wheel rim of his battle chariot and he will set his foot on every battlefield. He is moving towards battle now, and if you do not ward him off there will be endless destruction. It is he who seeks you in combat.'

'Who is he?' Maeve asked.

'He will lay low all your army and slaughter you in dense crowds. He will take all your heads. I will not conceal the truth from you. It is prophesied.'

'Who?' Maeve shouted.

'Blood will flow,' Feidelm said. 'Dead heroes will long be remembered. Men's bodies will be hacked. Women will lament …'

'Who is this warrior?' Maeve said, in a tone which brooked no refusal.

'His name is Cúchulainn,' Feidelm said.

3

The Two Faces of Cúchulainn

Cúchulainn, warrior and champion of all the world, put on his battle array. He began with twenty-seven tunics worn next to his skin. These were waxed, board-like and compact and were bound with strings and ropes and thongs close to his fair skin so that he would not become deranged when the rage came upon him. He tied the shirts very securely. There had been one cold winter's night during the hostings when, in his battle ardour, he had cast aside his twenty-seven constricting layers and the snow had melted for thirty feet around him and his charioteers had been forced to leave the furnace of his body.

Over the twenty-seven shirts he put on his hero's battle girdle of hard leather. It was tough and tanned and made from the best part of seven ox-hides of yearlings. It covered him from the thin part of his side to the thick part of his armpit; he wore it to repel spears and darts and lances and arrows. They glanced from it as though they had struck stone.

Around his loins he put on an apron of filmy silk, bordered with white gold, and outside that, to show to the world, he wore a dark apron of soft brown leather made from the choicest part of four yearling ox-hides and he fastened it with his battle girdle of cow's skins.

Dressed, the hero looked about him for his weapons. He chose the ivory-hilted, shining sword with eight little swords; he took his five-pronged spear with eight little spears; his javelin with eight little javelins, and finally eight little darts.

To protect himself he took eight shields together with his own special shield of dark red, big enough to shelter a prize boar within its curves. The rim of the shield was so sharp and razor-like that it would cut a hair against the stream and, when the battle raged, the hero could cut about him with the shield, or spear or sword. On his head Cúchulainn placed a crested war-helmet which cried aloud as from the throats of a hundred warriors. Goblins and demons and spirits of the glen circled around the helmet uttering shrieks and threats of bloodshed, and of the death of champion warriors. They followed him into battle and put fear and dismay into his enemies.

Over all this Cúchulainn threw a cloak about him. It was the protective dress brought to him from Manannán Mac Lir, from the king of Tír na Sorcha.

No ordinary man could have stood, let alone fought, in the heavy robes he chose to wear, but Cúchulainn was no ordinary man. When his ears caught the sound of coming conflict and his nostrils sniffed the scent of blood to be shed he became horribly distorted. His body grew mis-shapened and unrecognisable. His haunches shook like a tree in an autumn gale, or a helpless red against the current, and every limb and every joint and every member of his body shook with them. His body performed wild contortions within his skin. His feet and shins and knees came to the back; his heels and calves went to the front with the sinews sticking out of his shins each in a huge round knot the size of a warrior's fist. The muscles of his head were stretched to the nape of his neck and each vast, immeasurable, incalculable round ball of them was as big as the head of a month-old child.

His face became a red hollow. He sucked one eye into his head so deeply that a wild crane could not have reached in to pluck it out. The other eye sprang out on to his cheek. His mouth twisted into a fearsome shape and he drew the cheek back from his jawbone until his inner gullet was seen. His lungs and liver fluttered in his mouth and throat. He thrust his palate upwards with his fist and the fiery streams which came from his mouth were as large as the skin of a three-year-old sheep.

The beating of his heart was like the baying of a bloodhound, or a lion in full attack. The torches of the war-goddess were lit with the heat of his rage and sparks of blazing fire whirled around the cloud about his head. His hair curled like branches of red hawthorn and each single hair was strong enough and bristling enough to hold an apple impaled on its point. A beam of light – a hero's beam – shone like a hundred torches from his forehead, and a stream of dark red blood, as high and as thick and as strong as the mast of a great ship, rose from the top of his head to become a dark magical mist about him, and those who were near him on the eve of the battle saw him as a royal palace, brightly lit, but swathed in the mystery of winter's dusk.

Before the battle Cúchulainn called for his scythed chariot and the charioteer, his friend, Loeg, prepared himself too. He put on his hero's outfit but his was a tunic of soft deerskin, fine-textured and carefully stitched so that he could move his arms freely outside it. Over that he put on his raven-black cloak. Simon Magus had made it for the king of the Romans and Darius gave it to Conchobor and Conchobor gave it to Cúchulainn who gave it to his charioteer.

Loeg then put on his crested smooth four-cornered helmet, shot with all the colours of the spectrum and reaching protectively over his shoulders and down to the middle of his back. He wore it for effect and it was light enough not to hamper his movements. Around his brow he wore the distinguishing mark of a charioteer: a circlet of thin red-yellow gold, beaten into its narrow shape by a blacksmith on his anvil. In his right hand he took the spancel of his horses and his ornamented goad. In his left he grasped the driving reins.

The horses were protected by iron inlaid breastplates which were set with little spears and sharp points; the edges and wheels of the chariot were set with sharp lances in the same manner. The vehicle, armed thus, could cut a swath of destruction as Loeg drove it through the battlefield. Finally the charioteer cast a protective spell over the horses and over Cúchulainn so that they were invisible to everyone in the camp; they could see everything but could not be seen.

And then Cúchulainn sprang into the spiked chariot and rode triumphantly through the armies of the men of Ireland assembled against him. He killed two hundred in a thunder feat, and then three hundred, and then four hundred – but he stopped at five hundred. It was enough, he thought, for his first attack and the first contest, and so he directed Loeg to drive his chariot around the four great armies and, as he did so, the wheels cut into the ground so heavily that deep furrows, large enough to provide a fort and fortress and earthworks, were thrown up to prevent the enemy from fleeing from the battlefield. Cúchulainn wanted them there until he had taken his full revenge.

He cut across the middle of their ranks and threw up great ramparts of corpses and they fell, soles of their feet to neat headless necks in rows of six as he three times encircled them. No one has ever counted exactly how many fell that day. Common soldiers fell in their thousands and their chiefs with them. No less than three hundred royal kings were slaughtered and horses and hounds and women and boys and children and common folk lay dead beside them. Not one man in three of the men of Ireland escaped without a broken bone, or without being marked for life.

But the next day Cúchulainn came to see what had been done and to display himself to the women and girls, and to the poets and men of art. Wizardry had distorted him for battle and now he wished them to forget the monster and see his gentleness and beauty. And beautiful indeed he was. His hair glowed in three different colours: dark next to the skin, blood-red in the middle and over all a shimmering cloud of red-gold. A golden coil of hair was caught at the nape of his neck and the rest hung free about his shoulders. It was so pure in colour and so perfect in texture that no one had ever seen anything to compare with it. Around the nape of his neck it curled in a hundred red-gold twists and over his forehead were a hundred more. He had four dimples in each of his two cheeks: a yellow and a green, a blue and a purple. His eyes gleamed royally, each like seven brilliant gems and, unlike other men, he boasted seven toes on each of his feet and seven fingers on each hand, and each finger and each toe had the strength of a hawk's grasp and the grip of a hedgehog's claw.

Cúchulainn had dressed himself carefully for the occasion in a well-fitting fringed purple mantle, five-folded and caught with a brooch of white silver and inlaid gold. The brooch shone and winked in the morning sun like a bright piercing lantern on the darkest of nights. Next to his skin he wore a silk tunic, bordered with braid and fringes of gold and of silver and white bronze. It reached to the top of his dark-red soldierly apron of royal satin. He bore on one arm a splendid dark-purple shield rimmed with pure white silver and, on his left side, was a long grey-edged spear together with a sharp attacking dagger decorated with fine thongs and rivers of white bronze. Less beautiful were the nine heads he held in one hand and ten in the other to brandish in the face of his enemy as a token of his valour and conquest.

Maeve hid her head beneath a shelter of shields lest Cúchulainn should see her and attack, but the other women begged the men of Ireland to lift them so that they could see the vision, and the men made a platform of shields so that they could look and wonder at the beautiful youth in the chariot and compare him with the dark, twisted magical shape that had terrorised them the night before.

Only Dubthach Dael Ulad stood aside from the admiring crowd. He watched Cúchulainn displaying himself and his face blackened with anger and envy, and the men of Ireland nudged each other and said that it was on account of Dubthach's jealousy of his wife.

Dubthach got up and shouted at the crowd to lay an ambush around Cúchulainn and kill him.

'This is the man you saw last night!' he said, 'and he'll bring you nothing but mountains of corpses and weeping and misery. Your flesh will be fed to the ravens and the country will be littered with grave stones.'

Cúchulainn rode past him in triumph, ignoring him, and this brought Dubthach to a greater pitch of fury.

'Look – look at the severed heads he carries. Even now, dressed in his silken best, smiling at our women, luring them away from us – even now he isn't content without blood splashing about him.'

'Be quiet!' Fergus shouted.

Although he had spent many years in exile Fergus was still an Ulsterman. He rushed over to Dubthach and gave him such a strong and violent kick that he fell on his face beyond the crowd.

'Listen,' Fergus said, 'and watch.' His eyes swept around. 'Even Maeve is silent,' he said. 'She has come to wonder, not to fight.'

A flutter of excitement ran through the crowd and then there was a sigh, like the long drawn out breath of winter, as Cúchulainn circled around them once more, and then drove slowly out of sight.

4

The Death of the Bulls

Towards the end of what seemed like conflict, and while Cúchulainn was engaged in battle, Maeve's men took the Donn Cuailnge from his herdsmen. It was not an easy task. One herdsman made a stand at a narrow pass but Maeve's army drove the bull and cows towards him and they trampled him thirty feet into the ground and made small pieces of his body.

The men of Ireland brought the bull to Maeve and Ailill in their camp but there was little rejoicing. The bloodshed went on and on and, when both sides were almost reduced to nothing and the men of Ireland were in retreat to Connacht, Maeve sent the bull to Cruachú together with fifty of his heifers and eight messengers so that whether the army reached home or not, at least the Donn Cuailnge would arrive there as she had promised. Then her issue of blood came upon her and she sent Fergus to cover the retreat.

'By my conscience,' Fergus said, 'it is ill-timed.'

'I must pass my water,' Maeve said, 'or I'll die.'

Fergus complained bitterly but he came and covered the retreat of the men of Ireland and Maeve passed her water and it made three trenches in each of which a household could fit. Cúchulainn came upon her so engaged but did not wish to strike her from behind and Maeve, with a woman's wile, took the opportunity to ask him to let her army pass freely until they had gone westward past the Shannon.

'I grant it,' Cúchulainn said, and he not only let them pass but protected them.

Fergus surveyed the sorry sight as they travelled slowly westward. He sighed and went to Maeve.

'This is what happens when an army is led by a woman. You're like a mare leading a band of foals into unknown territory. There's no one to lead or counsel this army and that's why they were plundered and destroyed ...'

Maeve did not listen to him. She gathered what was left of the men of Ireland and went home to Connacht.

When the Donn Cuailnge saw the beautiful strange land he bellowed loudly three times. The Finnbennach, grazing peacefully on what he considered his own territory, heard him and tossed his head violently and came forward to Cruachú to meet him.

'There is going to be a fight,' the men of Ireland said to each other. No one was very anxious to watch. The bulls were dangerous and it was going to be a death-struggle.

There was a man in Cruachú called Bricriu. No one liked him very much. He had come to Fergus the year before begging for help because his goods had been stolen and Fergus, sorry for him, had taken him into his service. Bricriu had not, however, been grateful. He had insulted Fergus and picked a quarrel with him over a game of chess and Fergus, in a rage, had struck him so hard that one of the chessmen lodged in his head. During the whole war with Ulster Bricriu had been convalescing in Cruachú and it was only on the day of the army's return that he had got up from his sick bed.

'Bricriu can be the eye-witness,' someone said. 'He treats his enemies and friends equally badly – he'll do very well as a referee,' and Bricriu, very reluctantly, was brought to a gap in the fortifications behind which the men of Ireland were sheltering and was told to report on the battle of the bulls.

The bulls faced each other and pawed the ground. Earth flew up over their shoulders and down their backs and their eyes blazed like distended balls of fire. Their cheeks and nostrils swelled like bellows in a forge and they rushed towards each other and collided with a crashing noise. They began to gore and tear at each other and then the Finnbennach, with the advantage of being on home ground, and relying on the Donn Cuailnge's confusion after his travels, lunged sideways to the brown bull and thrust his horn into his side. Locked together they rushed violently to the spot where Bricriu stood and, before he could move, their hooves trampled him a man's length into the ground.

They stayed locked together, with the brown bull's hoof planted on the horn of the white one, for a full day and Fergus, tired of the inactivity, took his spear and slit the back of the Donn Cuailnge in three places.

'You're not much of a bull,' he said, striking home, 'the Finnbennach's only a calf but he's got the better of you.'

The Donn Cuailnge heard him clearly – was he not a human swineherd at one time? He roared with rage and attacked the Finnbennach with renewed strength. They fought long and loud until night fell and then all that the men of Ireland could do was listen to the noise and destruction. That night the bulls travelled the whole of Ireland, fighting over every inch of it. The next morning the men of Ireland went to see the result of the battle.

They saw the Donn Cuailnge coming past Cruachú from the

west with the Finnbennach a mangled mass on his horns but at first they could not decide which bull was which.

'Leave him alone,' Fergus said. 'Whichever it is – leave him alone in his triumph.' He paused. 'A mad bull – I have a feeling that whatever happened last night bears no comparison to what is going to be done now.'

The Donn Cuailnge came nearer. He stamped his foot and shook himself then turned his right side to Cruachú and left a heap of the Finnbennach's liver on the ground. He moved on to drink in Finnlethe and left the Finnbennach's shoulder blade behind him there, and then he came to the brink of the Shannon and left the loin of his enemy on the bank. And the place was called Áth Luain, the Ford of the Loins.

He travelled eastwards into Meath and there he left the rest of the Finnbennach's liver. He tossed his head fiercely and shook off the rest of the mangled bull over Ireland. He threw a thigh as far as Port Láirge, and his rib cage as far as Áth Cliath and after that he faced towards the north and home.

He recognised the land of Cuailnge. It was a land of weeping women and children lamenting the loss of their bull and he could hear them from far away. They recognised him too and stopped crying suddenly as the dim shape in the distance took on the familiar outline of his strong forehead and proud body.

But the Donn Cuailnge had indeed gone mad. He attacked the women and children who were there to welcome him and killed them in their hundreds. And when it was done he turned his back on their mangled bodies and set his face towards the hills. And his heart broke like a nut in his breast.

5

The Voyage of Maildún

Maildún slept in the same cradle as the other royal children, fed from the same breast and from the same cup, but he differed from any of them in this respect: he was more beautiful than any child that anyone had ever seen.

He was the favourite of the court and as he grew older and more handsome those around him found him to be generous and high-spirited. He behaved with great nobility too – it seemed there was nothing with which one could fault him. He lived the life of a prince in thee palace of the king and he won every prize in the games at court. There was no contest of skill, from chess to horseracing, in which he didn't take the palm. He was a golden youth, loved and admired, with the whole world at his feet.

It was hardly surprising, therefore, that he became the butt and envy of certain of his companions – it would have been surprising if he had not.

'It's not fair,' one of them said at the end of a particularly gruelling game, 'to be beaten by an outsider. A stranger …' He raised his voice. 'A fatherless stranger at that.'

There was a sudden sharp silence. Maildún stood perfectly still and let the ball fall from his hands.

'What do you mean?' he said, at last. 'Am I not the son of your king?'

'The son of the king!' The youth laughed. 'The son of no one you mean. We don't even know what tribe you belong to.' He paused. 'You just – appeared.'

Maildún stared at him and several sympathetic hands went to the hilts of their swords, but the moment passed and Maildún turned away and went in search of the queen.

'Why didn't you tell me?' he asked. 'You let me think I was your son.'

'No mother in the world could love her son as I love you,' she said.

'That is not an answer,' Maildún said.

'Yes it is,' the queen said. 'I love you – '

'As a son. But I am not your son, am I?'

She turned away and didn't answer. He put his hand to her face and made her look at him.

'I have just been called a bastard,' he said.

'No, no, you are not!' she said. Her face moved in anguish. 'You are the true son of a noble father.' She put out a restraining hand. 'Don't let anyone tell you that you are not! They are full of envy and – '

'Envy,' Maildún said, slowly. 'Then it's true. You are not my mother and the king is not my father.'

'Are you not happy with us?' the queen asked.

'You must tell me who I am!' Maildún said. His face was red and twisted with misery and anger.

'It won't bring you any happiness,' the queen said, gently.

'I have to know!' Maildún said. He paused. 'I can't eat or drink ...I can't live unless you tell me who my parents are.'

'It's foolish to delve into the past,' she said, and then she sighed as she saw the set of his jaw. 'Your father is dead. He died before you were born. You can't bring him back.'

'And my mother?' Maildún said. He looked at her eagerly. 'Is she still alive?'

'Yes,' the queen said. Her voice was very low. 'If you wish …if you wish, I'll bring you to her.'

She was not a queen for nothing. With great dignity she brought her beloved foster son to his real mother and joined their hands. Then she slipped away and left them alone.

Maildún and his mother had a great deal to say to each other. Maildún's world had been turned upside down in the last few hours, and his mother, who had never thought to greet him as a son, was completely overcome.

Eventually Maildún questioned her gently about his father.

'He's dead,' she said, tears in her eyes. 'His name was Ailill Ocar Aga and he was the chief of the tribe of Owenaght of Ninus, and a good man. When he was killed I brought you here for safety to the queen and …'

'Chief?' Maildún said.

'Our lands are beyond the Shannon,' his mother said.

'Chief?' Maildún said, again.

The next day he set out with his foster brothers – the king's three sons – to find his father's territory. His three brothers were noble and handsome like himself and when the people of the tribe found out who they were they had a royal welcome. They were feasted and feted and honoured, and it wasn't long before Maildún forgot all the humiliation and trouble of the previous weeks.

He forgot it enough to join a group of young people in a game of handstone. The game was to throw the stone clear over the charred roof of the nearby church. It had been burned many years before. Maildún played as well as any of them, indeed better than most, and once again, as the tall well-formed youth outshone his companions, there was someone watching, someone full of envy and resentment. His name was Brickna, a servant of the people who owned the church, and he was well known for his foul tongue.

'You should be out avenging the man who was burned to death here, instead of amusing yourself casting stones over his bare bones,' he said to Maildún.

'Who was burned here?' Maildún asked.

'Your father,' Brickna said, with satisfaction. 'He was killed by invaders who came by ship and burned him in this very church.'

'I didn't know,' Maildún said, sickened. 'Why did no one tell me?'

'Would you have listened?' Brickna said, looking the richly-clad Maildún up and down. 'You were enjoying yourself ...'

'I'll enjoy myself no longer,' Maildún cried. He dropped the stone he was holding, wrapped his cloak around him and buckled on his shield.

'The same pirates are still sailing the same fleet,' Brickna shouted after him.

'Then I'll find them!' Maildún said.

He left the company there and then – if he had a fault, it was impetuosity – and began to inquire of everyone he met where he might find the pirate ships. He wandered along the road, from house to house, from village to village, but no one could help him. At last someone told him that the fleet lay in a far off place and there was no reaching it except by sea. Maildún resolved immediately to build a curragh and to follow the men who had murdered his father and to avenge his death. His first task was to visit Corcomroe, in north-west Clare to consult the druid Nuca and ask his advice.

Nuca gave him explicit instructions. He told Maildún the exact day he should begin to build his curragh, and the exact day on which he was to set out on his voyage, and he was very particular about the number of crew which were to be sixty chosen men: no more, no less.

Maildún followed the druid's advice exactly. He built a triple-hide curragh, to Nuca's specifications, and chose his crew very carefully. Among them were his two great friends, Germane and Diuran Lekerd, and on the appointed day they set out.

The day was fair and all went smoothly until they looked back to the land and saw Maildún's foster brothers running along the shore and shouting, and waving at him to return and take them with him.

'We can't come back,' Maildún shouted, 'we have our exact number of sixty ...'

His words were lost on the wind and in any case his brothers were not listening. They had thrown themselves into the water and were swimming determinedly after the curragh.

'We'll follow you until we drown,' one called, arms flailing in the water, and Maildún sighed and directed that the curragh turn back and pick them up.

They sailed for two days, without sight of land, until at almost midnight of the second day they saw two small bare islands with two huge houses on them, near the shore. From the houses came the sounds of singing and laughter.

'Quietly,' Maildún said, and the curragh crept towards the shore until they could hear the voices clearly across the water.

'Warriors,' Maildún said, sharply.

They listened carefully and suddenly heard a man's voice raised in anger.

'Get out of my way! I'm the man who killed Ailill Ocar Aga – remember? No one can better that, especially you ...'

'It's the hand of God,' Germane whispered. 'We can creep ashore and kill them while they're feasting.'

Maildún nodded and gave the signal but, as they tensed themselves for battle, the wind blew up violently and drove them out to sea again and they had to run before the storm for all that night and for part of the next day. When the wind died down all navigation had been lost and they found themselves in a great ocean, far from the islands, and far, too, from home.

'Take down the sail,' Maildún said, calmly, 'and rest the oars. We'll let the boat drift, in God's hands.' He turned to his foster brothers. 'I should have listened to the druid. He said sixty men, not sixty-three. If we hadn't turned back for you ...' He glared at them. 'There'll be more trouble, you'll see. You can't fly in the face of a prophecy.'

His brothers shuffled their feet and gathered their cloaks around them, but didn't answer, and Maildún gave them another black look and then set to scan the horizon.

They drifted for three days and nights and shortly before dawn on the fourth day they heard the sound of waves breaking on a shore.

'Land,' Germane said, and they strained their eyes to see it. As soon as it was light they made towards it thankfully. The crew were suddenly cheerful again. They began to laugh and to cast lots as to who would be the first to go ashore. Even Maildún relaxed and began to smile.

Germane, sent forward to watch for rocks in the water, suddenly shouted a warning. Down the beach, eagerly awaiting the arrival of the curragh, ran a huge flock of ants, each one as large as a foal. They rushed over the red sand to the water's edge and jostled each other to get the first sight of the strangers. Their heads were sharp and intelligent and had all the signs of anticipating a good meal.

'They'll eat both crew and ship,' Diuran said, and turned the ship quickly and made out to sea again. Maildún's foster brothers averted their eyes from the frustrated ants, who were by now hopping up and down with rage, then they caught sight of Maildún's expression and averted their eyes again.

They didn't see land again for another three days and nights and when finally they saw, in the distance, a large high island with terraces of trees rising one behind the other they approached it cautiously. In the trees were perched great numbers of large brightly coloured birds.

'Food,' Germane said.

Maildún was not so sure. 'I'll go myself,' he said, and the king's sons offered to go with him. Fortunately for the morale of the crew they found the birds to be tame and, despite their beauty and friendliness, Maildún and his companions killed huge numbers of them and brought them back to the ship to be eaten.

It was rather a happier ship which set out the next day. One again they sailed without sight of land for three days and nights and came to another island on the fourth day. It was large and sandy and appeared to be inhabited solely by a huge animal who was standing on the beach. He was something like a horse in shape but with the legs of a dog, teeth like a saw, and great sharp blue claws. The animal was watching them intently and Maildún bid his oarsmen to row very slowly towards him. The monster seemed delighted as they came closer. He jumped and pranced with joy and lifted his nose up to the sky and bellowed – his reason being that he intended to eat the whole lot of them the moment they landed.

It was only at the last minute that Maildún realised their danger, and put back from the shore, and when the animal saw his supper retreating he ran in a rage to the water's edge and began to dig up large round pebbles with his sharp claws and fling them at the curragh.

'Another disaster,' Maildún said, looking at no one in particular, as they sailed out of reach of the monster.

Their next island proved to be broad and flat. It was Germane's turn to go ashore and he viewed the task very reluctantly but Diuran offered to go with him.

'That is if you'll agree to go with me when it's my turn,' he said, and Germane agreed.

The island was very large and they had walked some distance from the beach when they came to a broad green racecourse. There were huge indentations in the shape of hoof-marks in the turf.

'Looks as big as a ship's sail,' Diuran said.

'Or a dining table,' Germane said, nervously.

At the edge of the racecourse they found nut shells the size of helmets, and everywhere signs of a giant race only recently busily employed there.

Germane began to run and Diuran wasn't long in following him. They swam out to the curragh and hauled themselves on board, gasping for breath.

'Go and see for yourself,' was all they could say to Maildún.

Some of the crew, full of curiosity, went ashore in spite of Maildún's warnings but they were back within ten minutes and urging him to set sail. A few moments later they saw through the mist a crowd of enormous people rushing along the top of the waves, crying and screaming like demons. The giants tore up the shore and on to the racecourse and within minutes a race was in progress. The sailors, pale-faced, could hear great shouts going up like thunder as though they were close behind them.

'It seems the chestnut is winning,' Maildún said, dryly, and then: 'For God's sake make sail before the race is over, or we'll all be murdered as we stand.'

It was a week before they made land again: a week in which relations between Maildún and his foster brothers deteriorated greatly. Everyone on board was both hungry and thirsty and the crew were split into two factions, one which regretted that they had not tried to make friends with the giants, the other congratulating themselves on their narrow escape.

Maildún told his brothers flatly that they were haunted, and he made no bones about where he felt the fault lay.

It was a rather strained and very cautious group, therefore, who viewed the next island from the safety of the curragh. It was a high island with a large splendid house on the beach, quite near the water's edge. The house had two doors, one turned inland and the other towards the sea. The sea door was closed with a great flat stone and this stone had an opening through which the sea, beating against it, threw salmon into the house every day.

Hunger overcame fear and they landed and searched the house but they met no one. In one large room they found an ornamented couch intended for the head of the house, and in each of the other rooms were other couches with a crystal cup on a little table beside each one. The house was full of food and wine and brown ale and the sailors gave thanks, all quarrels temporarily forgotten, and ate and drank their fill. They lay luxuriously on the beautiful couches and drank from crystal and golden goblets, and admired the marble on the walls and the glittering dome of the house and, during all that time, they met no one nor heard any sound other than their own merry-making.

'Haunted?' asked the king's sons, as they set sail again.

Maildún frowned. 'I have heard of none of these lands,' he said, 'nor seen any ordinary signs of life.'

'There is no pleasing him,' one of his foster brothers said, giving a slight belch. 'That salmon was delicious.'

But sure enough, before many days had passed, the curragh was once again adrift, far from land, with a miserable and hungry crew aboard. They came at last to a tiny island which boasted nothing but a single apple tree in the middle of it. The branches were long and slender, and of even length and they reached down the hill as far as the sea. Unfortunately there was but a single apple on the tree. Maildún grabbed the branch as they went past and let it slide through his fingers.

'One apple,' the crew grumbled. 'What use is that?'

They circled the island for three days and nights, and all the time Maildún held the branch with the apple on it in his hands. At the end of the third day he found a cluster of seven apples on the end of it and each of these apples supplied them with food and drink for forty days and forty nights.

Thus refreshed, they were able to sail past the next island and observe its unpleasant occupants from a safe distance. The creatures resembled horses and, although the island was very beautiful, the nature of the animals was not. There were huge numbers of them and, as the sailors watched, they saw one take a huge bite out of its neighbour, who immediately did the same to the creature next to him. In a moment the entire herd was tearing and worrying each other until the ground was running with blood for miles around.

The next island, mercifully, had a high wall around it but, as they came near the shore, an animal of huge bulk with a thick leathery skin jumped over the wall and ran around the island with the speed of the wind. He came to a flat stone ready to take his daily exercise and, as Maildún and his followers watched incredulously, the animal turned himself round and round in his skin, the bones and flesh moving while the skin remained still.

After a while he stopped for a rest and then got up and shook himself and began the reverse process: turning his skin round and round his body while his bones and flesh stayed in place.

The next part of his programme was to run around the island again, as if to refresh himself. Then he went back to the same spot and, while keeping the skin of the lower part of body motionless, he whirled the skin of the upper part round and round like a millstone. It seemed that he spent almost all his time like this but his audience thought it best not to wait until the end of the show, and they hurried away and put out to sea. The monster, piqued, rearranged his bones and skin and ran after them intending to seize the ship but, finding them out of reach, began to fling large stones at them. He had a good aim and one hit Maildún's shield and went through it, lodging in the keel of the curragh. The last they saw of the animal were two huge eyes and an enormous open throat watching them hungrily from behind the wall as they sailed out of range.

Again, after some time, hunger overtook them.

'We're condemned to sail the seas forever,' Maildún said, in despair, 'and we'll never find the man who killed my father, and we will never see our families again.' He regretted the cool way in which he had treated his foster mother, and the hasty manner in which he had rushed from his real mother. Most of all he regretted not listening to the druid.

'This place is impossible,' Diuran said, as they came upon another beautiful island. 'Look at the pigs!'

The pigs – if pigs they were – were snuffing around and feeding from golden fruit which fell from the trees. From a distance it appeared idyllic but Diuran's sharp eyes had seen first what the others soon observed, to their absolute astonishment: the animals were bright red with fiery flames shooting out from and lighting up their bodies.

The pigs had a system of herding together and then rushing at the trunk of a tree and shaking it violently until the apple fell from it. These they ate and then proceeded to another tree. They kept themselves busy like this from dawn to dusk but at night they disappeared into caves and were not seen again until morning.

Around the island huge flocks of birds were swimming in the sea. As the pigs appeared for breakfast the birds swam away from the island. At noon, as though at a signal, they turned back and swam towards the shore again. They landed after the pigs had gone to bed and spread across the island, picking and eating the fruit from the trees as they went.

'If the birds can do it so can we,' Maildún said. He sent two reluctant scouts ashore after dark. They picked their way carefully up from the beach and found that the ground was hot to their feet.

'Carry on,' the crew shouted from the curragh. They were all hungry.

The scouts brought back a few apples and the men ate them greedily but were far from satisfied. Unfortunately by the time Maildún had found more volunteers to go ashore dawn was breaking and they had to wait until the next night before Maildún himself led a band to pick as much fruit as the vessel would hold.

But the apples did not last for long and it was only a few days before the crew, once again, were suffering from hunger and thirst.

'We should have picked more of the fruit,' one of his foster brothers said to Maildún.

'And sunk the curragh?' Maildún said. His brother didn't reply – he didn't want another lecture on the bad luck he had brought the ship – but he was one of the first to offer to go ashore when next they sighted land. It was a small island with a large palace on it, completely white, white all over without the smallest break or stain. It was as if it had been built of burnt lime or carved from an endless rock of chalk and, where it faced the sea, it was so high that it seemed to reach the clouds.

The whole was surrounded by an outer wall and a gate opened through it into a level courtyard. This was surrounded in its turn by more white houses, some of them were extremely grand indeed. Maildún and his shore party walked through the largest one and found several fine rooms, all quite deserted, but when they came to the main reception room they found it had one occupant: a small cat sitting on top of one of the square marble pillars which decorated the room. The cat looked at them coolly and then began to jump from the top of one pillar to the other. They assumed that they had interrupted its play and took no more notice of it.

The room itself was very ornate. Ranged around the walls were rows of precious jewels: brooches of gold and silver held to the walls by their pins, torques of gold and silver and, on a third row, great swords with jewelled hilts.

Couches were arranged around the room, white too but richly ornamented and tables were spread with the most delicious looking food. Maildún's brother pointed to a boiled ox and a roast hog and smacked his lips.

Maildún was hungry too, but the adventures they had on the enchanted islands had made him extremely wary. He approached the cat.

'Is that food for us?' he asked.

The cat stopped playing for a moment to listen to him and then gave him another cool stare and began to jump from pillar to pillar once more.

'I think that means yes,' Maildún said, nervously. 'We may as well ...er ...sit down.'

The feast included plenty of good strong ale and it wasn't long before the men were full of food and snoring their heads off. In the morning, yawning and groaning, they gathered up what was left of the meal and poured the remaining ale into one vessel and prepared to go back to the ship. Maildún's brother took a lingering look across the room.

'Shall I bring one of those torques with me?' he said.

'Certainly not,' said Maildún. 'We were lucky to sit down and eat instead of being attacked by one of their wild beasts – and in any case someone is sure to be watching.'

'Only a cat,' his foster brother said. 'A small, ordinary common or garden cat.'

'Take nothing,' Maildún warned him. He was becoming very tired of his foster brothers.

But the young man lingered behind when everyone else had gone, and then went back to the room and pulled one of the silver and gold torques from the wall. He hurried after the others, calling for them to wait as he crossed the courtyard to the wall facing the sea. The cat was on him in seconds. It had turned into a blazing fiery arrow and it pierced his body and reduced it immediately to a heap of ashes. Maildún turned and saw the cat resume its normal shape and go back to the pillar to resume his play once again. Gingerly Maildún went to pick up the torque and, skirting what was left of his brother, he returned the jewels to the inner room.

He spoke a few soothing and apologetic words to the cat, who seemed not to be listening, and then he put the torque in its place on the wall.

'Come on,' Maildún said, to the men who had followed him. He hurried back to the courtyard and bent to collect the ashes of his dead brother, expecting at any moment to feel a burning arrow in his back. The sailors went before him through the gate in the wall and down to the ship, their shoulders twitching in anticipation of attack but the cat, presumably still playing happily among his pillars, did not follow them. They set sail, sadly, and when they were well out to sea Maildún cast his brother's ashes over the dark water. His feelings were a mixture of anger and sorrow but he was not sure with whom he was more angry: his father's murderer for leading him on this dangerous voyage, his foster brother for ignoring his orders from the very beginning, or himself. There were a great many things, he felt, of which he could accuse himself.

Three days later, their hearts still heavy, they sighted land again and, almost as though it reflected their thoughts of death and mourning, the island was coloured mainly black and white. A brass wall, like the handles of a coffin, ran down the centre of the land and on either side of it were huge flocks of sheep. Those at one side were entirely black, at the other entirely white. A very large broad-shouldered man was dividing and arranging the sheep. From time to time he picked up a sheep and threw it effortlessly over the wall to the other side. When he threw over a black sheep it fell among the white ones and became white immediately and, in the same way, when he threw over a white sheep it changed to black.

Nobody on the curragh liked the look of the island at all. Maildún looked around for something to throw on to the island and found a black-barked stick. He aimed at the white side of the wall and, as he expected, it fell among the white sheep and turned white straight away.

'And that's what would happen to us if we landed,' Maildún said, calling the order to set sail. The crew turned almost as white as if they had been thrown among the sheep and they made as much speed as possible out to sea.

Three days later, as had become the pattern, they again made landfall. A herd of pigs were grazing near the shore. The crew killed one of them and made a fire on the beach to roast the meat. They all ate well, and then looked around to see what kind of land they had reached. To the centre of the island, which was broad and quite large, rose a high mountain. Diuran and Germane offered to climb it so as to see what lay on the far side.

'But be careful,' Maildún said, 'this place may appear friendly but – '

It did appear friendly. The plants and trees were familiar. The crew still had the delicious taste of roast pork in their mouths and the scent of it mingled with woodsmoke in the air gave them a sense of comfort and home.

Diuran and Germane set out and soon left the picnic party behind. The mountain was further away than they had realised and they were still some distance from it when they came to a broad shallow river. Germane sat down on the bank to rest and idly dipped the point of his lance into the water. The tip immediately burned off and Germane leaped to his feet in alarm.

On the other side of the river they saw a herd of huge, hornless cows and an equally huge man beside them. Germane began to bang his spear on his shield to rouse the cattle.

You're frightening my poor young calves!' the herdsman roared in a tremendous voice.

'Calves?' Diuran said. 'Calves?' The animals were enormous. Another thought struck him. 'Where are their mothers?' he asked.

'At the other side of the mountain,' the islander said. 'You can see for yourselves.'

The two friends hadn't the slightest wish to see for themselves. They were back on the boat with Maildún and the crew in a matter of minutes.

The next island was much nearer. It was the first time they had had their next sight of land while still having sight of the hills of the one they had left, blue and misty, to their stern. And there was something else. It was the first time they had found an island populated with ordinary people. At least they appeared to be ordinary. Men, in large crowds, led their horse-drawn wagons of corn to a huge mill. The miller was strong-bodied and burly and he stood in the doorway to his mill and watched carts and wagons coming towards him over the plains. Great herds of cattle covered the land as far as the eye could see and, when the sailors came nearer, they saw that although the nearest wagon held corn there were numberless other ones piled high with every kind of wealth: food and jewels, furniture and clothing, everything in fact which was ever coveted by man.

The miller took the goods as they came to him and everything from bushels of wheat to barrels of brilliant cascading jewels were put into the mouth of the mill to be ground. White spotted ermine, rich silk and red-gold ornamented couches, shields encrusted with huge rubies, cloaks of sable, drinking vessels of ornate design, pictures and tapestries, leather as soft as velvet and fleeces of wool as vast and as white as the travellers had ever seen all disappeared into the mouth of the mill and were ground into fine powder and, as the wagons were emptied, their owners turned and walked away westward.

'Who are you?' Maildún asked the miller, 'and why – ' He stopped and watched a particularly fine bolt of cloth as it was thrown into the mills.

'This is the Mill of Inver-tre-Kenand,' the miller said, 'and I am the Miller of Hell. Anything – any corn or any of the riches which men are dissatisfied with are sent here to be ground, and anything which anyone gains and tries to conceal from God – that is sent here too. And I grind them in the mill and send them afterwards to the west.'

He turned around and went back to his endless task and offered them no further explanation and Maildún and his men, also silent but very thoughtful, went to their curragh and sailed away.

Maildún's second foster brother had never really recovered from the loss of his brother. He spent a great deal of time lying down in the boat, refusing even to prepare the food. Sympathy was beginning to turn to resentment and, when they next sighted land, Maildún determined that his brother should go ashore. It would be good for him, he reasoned, and as well as that it might restore him in the eyes of the other men.

The island was again large and again well populated, but the people were black. They had black skin and black hair, black clothes and black headdresses and they walked about sighing and weeping and wringing their hands in an eternity of grief.

The young foster brother stood on the beach for a moment watching them but, within minutes, he had joined them and he too was walking up and down, crying and lamenting, his companions of the journey quite forgotten.

Maildún gritted his teeth and sent two others to find him and made a mental note to add bad judgement to the faults he had attributed to himself. The two sailors joined the crowd of mourners and searched in vain for the melancholy young man and it wasn't long before they too disappeared into the black mass of people and began to weep and mourn themselves.

'Four of you go,' Maildún said, grimly, 'and bring the others back by force if you have to.'

He gave them four spears and some short sharp knives and told them to cover their mouths and faces with their cloaks so as not to breathe the air of the country.

'And don't look either right or left or up at the sky or down at the ground. Concentrate on finding our men. That's all you're there for. Understand?'

They nodded.

'Are you sure you understand?' he said. 'Keep your eyes for finding your companions.'

With great trepidation they landed on the island and felt its air of gloom almost engulf them, but they remembered what Maildún had said and, for once, followed his instructions exactly.

'A miracle,' Maildún said to himself as he watched them from the curragh. They had wrapped themselves up as he had said and were searching diligently for the missing men. They found their two lost companions quickly. They were still weeping and wailing and they had to be brought back by force, but of Maildún's foster brother there was no sign at all.

'And why did you weep?' Maildún asked, when they had recovered somewhat.

'No reason,' they said. 'We did what everyone else was doing.'

They searched again for the sad young brother, but he had disappeared completely.

'Or turned into a black-faced mourner,' one of the crew – the one who had had to take the foster brother's share of the work on the curragh – said spitefully.

'We have to leave,' Maildún said, and turned his face from the sounds of weeping. He looked at the endlessly moving sea and thought of his childhood days with the sons of the king. He had called them brothers and now two of them were lost forever. And he thought of the druid Nuca and of the warning he had ignored and, once again, he saw his foster brothers swimming out after the curragh. Surely, he said to himself, things will go better now, we have been punished enough. And then he pushed aside the thought as selfish: it was after all his brothers who had been sacrificed, not he.

Four walls, meeting in the centre, divided the next island. The first was of gold, the second of silver, the third of copper and the fourth wall of crystal. In the first division were kings, in the second, queens, in the third, youths, and in the fourth, young girls. They landed, by tacit agreement, on the fourth part of the island.

One of the maidens came to meet them and led them to a house. She brought out some food in a small vessel. It looked like a kind of unappetising cheese and they took a little of it, cautiously, but to their surprise each found that it tasted of his own particular favourite food. They asked for more and went on eating and eating from the very same small vessel until they were satisfied. Then they fell into a sweet intoxicated sleep and slept for three days and three nights and, in the depths of his dreams, Maildún thought that indeed his bad luck was at an end.

But when they woke on the third day they found themselves in the curragh on the open sea and there was no sight in any direction of the gold and silver walls, or of the young maiden, or indeed of the island itself.

It seemed a long way to the next island. Germane was the first to sight it.

'There is a palace,' he said, excitedly, 'but it is small. And ...oh, there is a fountain in front of it and a bridge made of crystal, and a copper chain hangs in front of the building, and there are silver bells hung upon the chain and ...there is a beautiful young woman.'

'We'll row ashore,' Maildún said.

They tried to cross the crystal bridge which spanned the fountain but each time they put a foot on it they fell backwards on to the ground. The young woman came out of the palace as they scrambled awkwardly to their feet. She lifted a crystal slab from the bridge and filled her pail from the fountain and then went back into the palace again.

'This woman has been sent to keep house for Maildún,' Germane said. He was still in an elated condition from their last island.

'Maildún indeed!' said the young woman, slamming the door of the palace.

The crew began to shake the copper chain and the silver bells made a soft, tinkling sound and the men forgot their anxiety to get into the palace and sat down and nodded their heads sleepily. Before they knew it they woke up and found that it was morning.

The young woman came out of the palace again with her pail and once more lifted the crystal slab to draw water.

'She's certainly meant for Maildún,' Germane said, staring.

'Wonderful Maildún,' she said, and the closing of the door echoed the sharp tone of her voice.

But they stayed on, hopefully, for three days and three nights and, each morning, the girl came out and filled her pail from the fountain. But on the fourth day she came towards them, beautifully and regally dressed. Her bright yellow hair was bound by a circlet of gold and she wore silver-work shoes on her small white feet. More silver caught her white cloak at her throat and underneath the cloak, next to her soft white skin, she wore a dress of thin fine silk.

'My love to you, Maildún,' she said, holding out her hand. She went from one man to the next, mentioning all of them by name and offering them all her love. 'We knew that you were coming to our island,' she said. 'It was in a prophecy – '

And she took them to a large house by the sea and instructed them to draw the curragh high on to the beach. In the house were a number of couches. One was for Maildún; the others were each to be shared by three. The woman gave them food, once again a cheese-like substance in a small vessel and, once again, they each found in it whatever taste they wished. Afterwards she lifted the crystal slab from the fountain and drew water for them to drink and, each time, she knew exactly how much each man would eat or drink; she gave them exactly that and no more.

'She would make Maildún a good wife,' the men said, but when she heard that she picked up her pail and left them alone.

'Shall we ask her?' Germane said to Maildún'

'Ask her what?' Maildún said.

'To be your wife.'

'And how will that be of any advantage to you?' Maildún said, but he lay back on his couch with a happy smile on his face.

She came the next morning and they put the question to her.

'Stay and make friends with him,' Diuran said. 'Get to know us all. He will make a fine husband.'

'We are not allowed to marry sons of men,' she said. 'And no one on this island can disobey.' She left them then and went back to her house but came as usual the following morning and gave them food and drink. And, as usual with food and drink, they became more cheerful and put the question to her again.

'Tomorrow,' she said. 'Tomorrow I'll give you an answer.' She smiled and left them once more and they curled up on their couches and went to sleep.'

When they awoke they were afloat in the curragh near to a great high rock. The woman and the palace and the crystal bridge and the island, like the island of the four precious walls, had completely disappeared. To the north-east they could hear a confused murmur of voices and they steered towards the sound. Soon hills and mountains came into view and they saw that this new land was full of birds, some black and some brown and some speckled. It was the birds who were making the clamour. They were shouting and calling each other in human voices so loudly that Maildún and his companions were almost deafened. They did not land but made their way to the next island which lay nearby.

There were birds, too, on this one and many trees. The island was small and, on the shore, looking at them, they saw a very old man. He was covered from head to foot in long white hair, and wore nothing else. They landed and asked him who he was.

'I am a man of Erin,' he said, 'and many years ago I put out to sea in a small curragh to go on a pilgrimage, but the vessel was very unsteady and I put back to land and cut green sods of turf from my own country to act as ballast in the boat, and then I set out again.' The old man smiled. 'And God was very good to me. When I arrived at this spot he fixed the sods of turf in the sea for me, so that they formed a little island and, although there was scarcely room for me to stand, I came ashore and made my life here. And every year God has added a foot to the length and to the breadth of the island until now it is a comfortable size. And as the island has grown, so have I aged.

'And the trees?' Maildún asked.

'God caused a single tree to grow each year,' the old man said, 'and now the island is covered with trees – as I am covered with hair.'

'And the birds?' Diuran said.

'They are the souls of my children and all my descendants, men and women alike,' the old man said. 'They are sent to live with me here when they die in Erin.' He paused and looked at their surprised faces. 'We have plenty of food,' he said. 'God has made a well of ale to spring up and every morning the angels bring me half a cake, a slice of fish and a cup of ale from the well and, in the evening, the same is given to everyone of my people. And we live like this and we will go on living like this until the end of the world.' The old man sighed and then added, 'we are waiting for the day of judgement.'

But he was able to feed the voyagers and treated them hospitably for three days and three nights until they were well rested and ready to set out again. He stood on the shore and waved to them.

'You will reach your own country again,' he said to them, 'all but one man.' And his words were snatched by the wind and echoed around them.

They ran into a storm and were tossed about for days, quite helplessly. Maildún began to doubt the old pilgrim's prophecy. If any of them got back to Ireland, he thought, they would be fortunate indeed. The crew were cold and hungry and, when they finally sighted land, they were eager to go ashore but Maildún heard a great roaring noise and big voices and the sound of smiths' hammers striking iron on an anvil. Each blow sounded like a dozen hammers and he told the crew to move in slowly over the breakers and to listen carefully.

They didn't need to strain their ears. The smiths' voices boomed out over the water.

'Are they near?' one smith asked. The watchers in the boat were being watched from the shore.

'Shsh – listen,' another smith said.

'Who are they?' the first one asked.

'Pigmies. Little fellows rowing towards the beach in a toy boat,' said the second.

Maildún didn't wait to hear any more.

'Put back to sea,' he yelled, 'but don't turn the curragh or they'll realise we've heard them. Reverse your oars!'

They did as he said without losing the rhythm of their stroke – they had seen the giant smiths too by then – and the boat moved smoothly backwards, as though it were flying over the waves.

The smiths watched them carefully.

'They aren't getting any nearer,' one said, at last.

'But they haven't turned their boat; they seem to be resting,' said the other.

They watched for another few minutes.

'What are they doing now?' the first one asked.

'I think they're flying!' the look-out said. 'They're further away than they were –'

The first smith rushed out of the forge in a rage. He was a huge giant of a man and in his right hand he held tongs which carried a vast mass of glowing iron. He ran down to the shore and flung the red-hot mass at the curragh. It fell a little short but near enough to cause the whole sea to hiss and boil and throw the boat around in the water, but they quickened their stroke and were out of reach before he had time to throw anything else.

The sea changed. It was like green crystal, smooth and calm and transparent after the storm. They could see the sand at the bottom quite clearly, sparkling in the sunlight. There were no rocks, no seaweed, no fish, no monsters of any kind, just the clear bright water and the gleaming sand. They sailed for a whole day simply looking at the sea and they forgot that they were hungry or that they were lost, or that they were searching for the men who had killed Maildún's father.

The sea changed again, becoming thin and clear and cloudlike. It was so light that they didn't think it would hold the weight of the curragh and, beneath then, through the clear water, they could see a beautiful country with huge mansions surrounded by groves and woods. One large single tree stood some distance from the settlement and in its branches a fierce animal crouched. The animal was watching a herd of oxen grazing nearby; a herdsman, armed with a shield and spear, guarded them and the crew of the curragh realised that he hadn't seen the tree monster. As they watched he looked up, took one terrified look at the tree and ran for dear life, leaving his shield and spear after him. The monster, spurred into activity, stretched his fangs and plunged them into the back of the largest beast, lifted it off the ground and swallowed it whole. The entire incident took only seconds and within another second the rest of the herd had taken flight. Maildún and his crew were left alone with the monster and only the thin, mist-like sea between them. They moved forward very slowly and with great difficulty, taking care not to disturb the water too much, until finally they crossed the thin sea safely and reached their next island.

They were fated not to land there. A huge wall of water rose on all sides of the island, forming a rigid circle; within it the inhabitants were rushing backwards and forwards in alarm, shouting that invaders had come.

'They've come to raid us again,' they cried, and they drove their huge herds of cattle and horses and sheep away from the shore. One woman began to throw large nuts at the curragh. The nuts curved over the wall of water and landed to float on the waves around the boat, and the crew gathered them in enormous quantities and kept them to eat later.

They turned the boat to go away and, as they did so, they heard someone shout that the invaders were going. There was relief in his voice.

'Quite a change,' Maildún said, 'from being attacked ourselves at each and every turn. They must have been expecting their enemies.'

Tiring of a diet of nuts, albeit ones they hadn't had to collect for themselves, they were thankful to find another source of food on the next island which they visited. From one beach rose a huge fountain of water. It spanned the breadth of the island, in the form of a rainbow, and landed on the beach on the other side. Maildún and his men walked under it without getting wet – not only that: they hooked huge quantities of salmon from it. Before long the salmon were falling down of their own initiative and after a few hours of this there was a distinct smell of fish everywhere and the crew were up to their knees in twitching fins. For twenty-four hours the stream held its shape, flowing from one side of the island to the other like a solid arch. Maildún told the sailors to fill the curragh with fish.

'Quickly,' he said, holding his nose, 'and let's move on.'

'I can see something,' Diuran said, when they had sailed for a full day, 'but if it's an island, it's a very strange one.'

It was not an island. It was a huge silver octagonal pillar standing, apparently unsupported, in the sea. Each side was the width of one oar-stroke and its base was buried deep in the ocean floor, far below. It quivered, bright and shining, up into the sky and they couldn't see the top but a silver net hung down from it and reached as far as the water. Its meshes were so large that the curragh in full sail passed through one of them and, as they did so, Diuran struck the mesh with his sword and cut a piece off it.

'Don't destroy it!' Maildún said. 'It must be the work of great men.'

'I did it for God,' Diuran said. He paused. 'And so that they might believe us then we go back home – I will take it to the high altar in Armagh.'

The piece of silver was afterwards found to weigh two and a half ounces.

Before they sailed out of reach of the silver pillar they heard cheerful sappy voices coming from the top of it, but the language was unknown to them and they sailed on, no wiser than before.

They came to another pillar, supporting a small island which they named 'Ecnos' or 'one foot'. They rowed around the pillar and could see no way to land but, at the foot of the pillar, deep in the water, they saw a door which was securely bolted and they decided that this must be the only way in.

'Does anyone live here?' Maildún shouted, over and over again, but they got no reply, only the sound of the waves and the wind.

'I have a longing,' Maildún said, 'to meet some ordinary human people.'

They were all tired. Their minds were blunted by the strange places they had visited and their bodies were weary from many months at sea and from alternate weeks of hunger and rich diet. Germane, in particular, was heartily tired of salmon. It was with great relief, then, that they found their next landfall to be a large, inhabited island. At one side rose a high, heath-clad mountain, but the rest of the land was grassy and flat. A high palace stood near the shore. It was beautifully carved and decorated with precious stones and was defended by a high rampart around it.

Maildún and his sailors went towards it hopefully and sat down to rest near the outer gateway of the fortifications. They looked through the open door and saw a large number of lovely young girls inside and, as they looked, they heard the sound of hoof-beats and another girl rode towards them on horseback. She was beautiful and very richly dressed in a silver-fringed purple cloak with a blue silk headdress. Her gloves were interwoven with gold and her small feet were laced with scarlet sandals. One of the girls came out and held her horse as she dismounted and then they went into the courtyard, not without a keen glance at the newcomers.

After a few moments a girl was sent out to invite Maildún and his companions into the palace and they realised the beautiful rider in the rich clothes was the queen of the island.

She made them welcome and took them to a large room where a good meal was waiting for them. Maildún was served with his own dish of choice food and a crystal goblet of wine; his men shared large plates of food in threes, but all had plenty to eat. Afterwards they slept on soft couches and didn't wake until the morning.

The queen sent for Maildún again the next day.

'Will you stay with us?' she asked. 'Give up your long voyage from island to island. You'll stay young here, and you'll never know illness or pain – only pleasure.'

'And how do you spend your days?' Maildún asked, cautiously.

'That's easily told,' the queen said. 'My husband was the king of this island and these girls are our children. He's dead now – after a good reign – and we have no son, so I rule in his stead. And every day I go to the Great Plain to administer justice among my people.'

'And must you go today?' Maildún asked.

'Every day,' the queen said, 'but you may stay here, in this house, and I will come back to you in the evening.' She smiled at him. 'There is nothing for any of you to do but rest.'

And rest they did for three long months. Maildún settled into the life very quickly, but to Germane the months felt like three long years and many of the crew were openly grumbling.

'We want to go home,' they said, coming to Maildún with a petition.

'Home?' Maildún said. He was lying on a couch and his words were smothered by a yawn. He had also put on a little weight. 'Where could we find anywhere so comfortable as this place?' he asked.

There was a sharp exclamation, quickly suppressed, from the back of the group.

'All right,' Germane said, calmly. 'You're in love with the queen – so you stay here, but the rest of us are going back to Ireland.'

'Ireland?' Maildún said. He heaved himself to a sitting position. 'Ireland – ' he said dreamily. He stood up. 'We'll go together,' he said, 'or not at all.'

Two or three days later, while the queen was busy with her daily dispensation of justice on the Great Plain, they got the curragh ready and put out to sea, every last man of them, but they hadn't gone far before the queen, riding back to the palace, spotted them out at sea. She hurried into the palace and came back with a ball of thread in her hand.

She walked down to the water's edge and threw the ball after the curragh, but kept the end of the thread in her hand. Maildún caught the ball as it was passing and it clung to his hand and the queen, gently pulling the thread towards her, was able to draw the boat back to the harbour. They landed, reluctantly, and she made them all promise that if this should happen again someone would stand up in the curragh and catch the ball.

Nine long months passed during which the crew made several attempts to escape but each time the queen brought them back by means of the thread, Maildún always being the one to catch the ball.

Diuran, grimly, called a meeting and everyone agreed that the fault lay with Maildún.

'He's still in love with thee queen,' Germane said, 'otherwise why would he always catch the ball and make sure that we had to go back to the palace?'

'All right,' Maildún said, 'let someone else catch the ball next time,'

They waited for an opportunity and the next time the queen was away they again put out to sea. As always the queen arrived back before they had gone far and she threw the ball towards the boat. Another man caught it – Maildún was held back by his companions – but the ball stuck to his hand too and gently, inexorably, they found themselves being drawn back to the island.

Diuran, furious, jumped up and cut off the man's hand with his sword. It fell, with the ball of thread, into the sea.

'Row!' Diuran cried. 'Row as fast as you can!'

They pulled out to the open sea and when the queen saw that she had lost she began to weep and wring her hands and tear her hair; the other girls began to cry too and the whole place was full of tears and cries of misery.

'Row!' Diuran said, 'and look that way!' He pointed to the distant horizon.

They did row and they kept their eyes averted from the wailing behind them and eventually the cries became fainter and the island dropped out of sight of their stern.

It is said that for every disease there is a cure, and so it proved. For a long time they were tossed about in heavy seas, with Maildún, morose and gloomy, in the stern, but eventually they came to a wooded island. The trees on it resembled hazels and carried a strange fruit, not too different in appearance from apples, but having a rough, berry-like skin.

Some volunteers went ashore and picked all the fruit from one small tree and brought it back to the boat. There was a heated discussion as to who should try it and eventually Maildún said that would be the one. He took some of the fruit and squeezed the juice into a cup and drank it. A few minutes later he passed into a deep intoxicated coma and lay, with the red juice still foaming on his lips, neither moving nor appearing to breathe until the next day.

The crew thought that he was dead but, exactly twenty-four hours after he had drunk the juice, Maildún awoke and said that there was nothing in the world like it. He told them to pick as much fruit as they could carry and fill the curragh with it.

This was another occasion when they did exactly as they were bid; under Maildún's instructions they pressed the gathered fruit until every one of their vessels was full of juice but it was so strong that they had to mix large quantities of water with it before they dared to drink it.

Fortified, they sailed on and came once more to land. This island was larger than most of those they had seen. One side grew oaks and yew trees, the rest was a grassy plain with a small lake in the middle of it. A fine house stood beside a small church and flocks of sheep grazed nearby.

There was a hermit in the church, an old man with a snow-white beard and a face marked heavily by time.

'I am one of the fifteen who followed the example of our master, Brendan of Birra,' he told the sailors. 'We came on a pilgrim voyage and eventually settled here on this island, but the others are dead now. I am the last one left.' And he showed them Brendan's satchel, which the pilgrims had brought with them, and Maildún kissed it and they all bowed down in veneration.

'You may stay here,' the old man said, in a quavering voice, 'and eat what you wish.' He paused. 'But waste nothing.'

Some days later, as they were sitting on a hill and gazing out to sea, they saw what appeared to be a black cloud coming from the south-west. It came nearer and they saw that it was in fact a huge bird with heavy, black, flapping wings. They watched it warily – it was big enough to catch a man in its talons – while it circled wearily and then landed on a small rise beside the lake. Maildún signalled them to hide and they watched it from the cover of rocks and trees. The bird was very old and he held in one claw a tree branch which was heavier and thicker than the largest full-grown oak. He had brought the branch across the sea and it was covered with fresh green leaves and rich red fruit, rather like grapes but larger.

The bird rested on the hill for a while and then began to eat the fruit from the branch. The sailors had been watching him for a long time now and he had shown no signs of attacking them so they moved up closer and then, led by Maildún, circled him with their shields raised. Then one of the men went right up to the bird and took some fruit from the branch, but the birds went on eating and took no notice of him.

Evening came and the men were resting and looking out over the sea to the south-west when they saw what appeared to be two more black clouds coming towards them. The clouds were two more birds, younger and not quite as large as the first one. They flew at a great height, nearer and nearer, until they reached the hillock, and then they swooped down and landed, one on either side of the older bird.

They appeared to be very tired. They rested for a long time but then, refreshed, they shook their wings and began to pluck the old bird all over, pulling out the decayed quill points and the old feathers and smoothing his plumage with their beaks. When they had finished grooming him to their satisfaction they all three picked some more fruit from the branch and settled down to a good meal.

The next morning the birds began to pick at the tattered feathers of the older bird. They worked on him until midday and then, as before, they began to eat the fruit from the branch, throwing the stones and what they did not eat of the fruit into the lake. Slowly the water turned red like wine and the old bird plunged into it and swam and washed himself in it and swam again. He stayed in the water until evening when once again the sailors saw him being groomed by the younger birds in the warm light of the setting sun. This time they had perched on a different part of the hill, as though to get away from the mess of feathers and old quills which they had left behind earlier.

On the third day the two young birds resumed the picking and smoothing of the old one's feathers. They worked even more carefully, arranging the plumes in beautiful and glossy tufts and ridges and they worked, as before, until midday. When they had rested for a while they opened their wings and stretched them and then flew away into the south-west, and the crew of the curragh lost sight of them.

The old bird continued the job they had started, shaking his own feathers and smoothing them carefully. He worked until evening; then, he too stretched his wings and flew up into the air. He flew three times around the island, as if to try his strength. He had lost all the signs of old age. His feathers were thick, his eye bright and his head erect and he flew with the power of the younger birds. He alighted for the last time on the hill and then, after a short rest, he flew away to the south-west in the wake of his companions.

'That bird,' Maildún said, 'is young again.'

'"Thy youth shall be renewed as the eagle"' Germane muttered, remembering the words of the prophet.

'If we bathe in the lake too,' Diuran said, eagerly, 'we'll all be young again.'

The crew were not enthusiastic.

'How do you know the bird didn't leave his old age behind in the water? You might pick that up instead,' one of them said, but Diuran wasn't listening.

He threw off his clothes shouting that they could please themselves but he was going in. He swam about for a while and swallowed some of the lake water.

'Come on in,' he shouted, but they stood on the bank and watched him until he grew tired and climbed out again.

He dried himself and they saw that he was still sound; from that day Diuran never lost a tooth, or had a grey hair, or any illness of any kind – but no one else in the group had the courage to venture in.

Rested, and – in Diuran's case – renewed – they filled the curragh with mutton, said goodbye and gave their grateful thanks to the old pilgrim and put to sea once more.

Maildún was beginning to think that perhaps their troubles were over – the islands were becoming less hostile, some indeed were quite welcoming – and, when they reached the next landfall and saw a vast plain full of people laughing, he asked the crew to draw lots as to who would go ashore. It fell to the youngest of his foster-brothers; the quiet one who had not troubled Maildún during the voyage as his brothers had done.

The minute he landed he went towards the lively, laughing people as if he had known them all his life and before another minute was up he had joined them in their game.

The men watched anxiously from the curragh, waiting for him to come back to report, but he never looked in their direction. He had been swallowed up by laughter as his elder brother had been overcome by despair.

They waited in the curragh for a long time. No one wanted to go after him – they feared that they too would not come back.

'He and his brothers put a curse on us,' someone muttered and, at last and with heavy heart, Maildún remembered the first old man they had met – the pilgrim on his island of birds and trees – and that he had told them that they would all get home safely, all except one. With great sadness in his voice Maildún told the crew to set sail and leave his foster brother behind. Perhaps now, he thought, they were rid of all the curses and prophecies and would sail safely home to Erin.

But it was not to be. They came next to a land entirely surrounded by a wall of fire. The wall revolved around the island and in it was one large open door. As the wall turned the sailors caught a glimpse of what lay inside. Richly dressed, beautiful people were feasting and laughing. They drank from embossed vessels of red gold and they radiated happiness such as the travellers had never seen. The sound of singing came gently across the water and Maildún stayed the curragh, his spirits soaring. They watched and listened through the night and felt a comfort like the ease which follows pain.

'Blessed are they – ' Germane said, but they did not venture to land within the ring of fire.

The next day they saw something floating in the water and thought at first that it was a huge white bird. It rose and fell on the waves but when they turned the curragh towards it they saw it was a man standing on a broad bare rock. The man was very old and covered all over with long white hair. He continually threw himself on his knees and never stopped praying.

They asked for his blessing and he gave it and then they asked him how he came to be there. The old man told them the following story:

'I was born and bred on the island of Tory and, when I was old enough, I joined the monastery.' The old man looked away, 'I became the cook and I was a very wicked man. I sold food entrusted to me and bought jewels and finery with the money and then – even worse – I made a secret passage into the church, underground, and also into the houses around and I used to steal church treasure.' The old man paused again and Maildún and his crew stayed quiet, waiting for him to tell the rest. Sea birds wheeled overhead, crying loudly; the waves roared on to the rock and when the old man began to move his lips again they had to come close to hear him.

'I became very rich,' he said, in a low voice. 'I filled my rooms with couches and linen and woollens, and brass pitchers and gold brooches. I had everything that those of rank had, and I became very proud.

'One day I was sent to dig a grave for the body of a farmer. I found a spot in the little graveyard on the island and began to dig but, as soon as I'd broken the ground, I heard a voice coming from under my feet.

'"Do not dig this grave!" it said, and I dropped my tools, terrified.

'There was no further sound and I decided that I'd imagined the voice so I began to dig again, but as soon as I picked up the spade it spoke again.

'"Don't dig this grave! I am a holy person and my body is lean and light and I don't want that fat, pampered, sinful farmer down on top of me."

'"I'm going to dig the grave!" I shouted back. Pride had overcome fear. "And I will bury the body on top of you!"

'"Then the flesh will fall off your bones; you will die in three days and go to the eternal pit – you know where that is?" the voice said. "And what's more, the body won't stay where you put it."

'I paused. "And if I don't bury it on top of you – what will you give me?"

'"Everlasting life in heaven."

'I paused again. What I had on this earth was real and solid. I was not eager to take the word of a disembodied voice coming from under the ground.

'"How can I be sure – and how do you know?" I asked.

'"Look at the grave," the voice said. "It's clay, isn't it?"

"Yes," I said.

"Then watch carefully," the voice said, "and if the clay changes, then you will know what I say is true. It will all happen the way I say that it will. You cannot bury the man on top of me."

'I didn't have to wait for proof. The clay turned into white sand in that very instant. I didn't stay to argue with the voice any longer. I took away the corpse and buried it somewhere else.

'Some time after this I had a new curragh made. Oh – she was a lovely thing! The hides were painted all over red and she was the sweetest boat you ever saw. I sailed along the shores and among the islands and I so liked the view of the world from the sea that I decided to live on the water for a while. I brought all my treasures, my silver cups and gold bracelets and drinking horns and everything else I had stored away, and I made myself comfortable in the curragh and sailed up and down along the coast.

'It was very pleasant for a while. The air was clear and the sea was calm and smooth and I enjoyed myself enormously but one day the wind blew up and, before I knew it, I was in the centre of a storm and being carried out to sea. I completely lost sight of the land and I had no idea where I was drifting. When the storm died down the sea was quite smooth again and the curragh sailed along as before but I was quite lost.

'Suddenly, to my surprise, the curragh stopped even though the breeze was still blowing and I stood up to see what had happened. I saw an old man, not far away, sitting on the crest of a wave.

'He spoke to me and I knew that I'd heard his voice before and, even though I couldn't remember where I had heard it, I began to tremble.

'"Where are you going?" the old man asked.

'"I don't know," I said, "but now that the storm is over and my boat is safe I am quite happy."

'"You wouldn't be," he said, "if you could see the troops surrounding you."

'"What troops?" I said, alarmed.

'"All around you, as far as you can see to the horizon, and above you up to the clouds, is a great towering mass of demons – "

'"Demons?" I said.

'"Yes, demons." He paused. "Summoned by your greed, and your pride and all your other sins and vices."

'I couldn't answer him.

'"Do you know why your curragh has stopped?" he said.

'"No," I said.

'"I stopped it," he said, "and it won't move until you promise to do exactly what I ask."

'"I can't do exactly as you ask," I said, hotly.

'"Oh yes you can," he said, "and if you don't all the demons and torments of hell will swallow you up."

'He came closer to the curragh, close enough to put his hand on me and make me swear to do what he demanded.

'"First," he said, "throw all the treasures you have in the curragh into the sea."

'"Into the sea?" I said. "All those precious things – just throw them away?"

'"They won't be lost," he said. "Someone will come and take care of them. Now – do as I say."

'I looked around. "I can't see any demons," I said. I picked up an ornate silver cup and weighed it in my hand.

'"Nor can you see what's holding me up in the water," he said, pleasantly.

'I sighed, and threw the cup overboard.

'"That's better," the old man said. "And now the rest of them, quickly."

'I tried not to look as the lovely gold and silver vessels and ornaments slid down out of sight into the dark water.

'"You can keep the wooden drinking cup," the old man said, and watched implacably until that was all that I had left.

'"Now," he said, "you can continue your voyage, but the first solid ground you reach – there you must stay."

'He gave me seven cakes and a cup of thin whey and then released whatever was holding the curragh and I sailed on. Within minutes he was out of sight. It was only then that I remembered that his voice was the voice I had heard coming from the grave.

'I was so upset and frightened by this, and by all that I'd lost, that I threw away the oars and gave myself up to the wind and currents. I was tossed about and blown back and forth and I lost all track of time but, after what must have been days, once again the curragh stopped moving.

'I stood up as before and, as before, I could see no sign of land, but when I looked up more carefully I saw near me a very small rock, just level with the surface of the water. Waves seemed to spring back and the rock rose high over the level of the sea and as I stood there, helplessly, the curragh drifted by and disappeared from view. I haven't seen it from that day to this, and this rock has been my home ever since.

'For the first seven years I lived on the seven cakes and the cup of whey which the old man had given to me; when the cakes were finished I went hungry for three days and had nothing but whey to wet my lips. On the evening of the third day an otter brought me a salmon out of the sea but, even though I was very hungry, I couldn't bring myself to eat raw fish so I threw it back into the waves.

'I was without food for another three days and then, once again, in the evening, the otter came back with the salmon. And I saw another otter bringing firewood. He piled it up on the rock and blew on it until it caught fire and lighted. And I broiled the salmon and ate and ate until I was satisfied.

'The otter brought me salmon every day – ' the old man went on but, at this point in the narrative, Germane began to groan, remembering all the salmon, raw and cooked, which he had eaten since they set out; Maildún hushed him and told the holy man to continue his story.

'I lived for seven years like this,' the old man went on, 'the otter bringing me a salmon a day and the rock growing daily larger until it became its present size.

'At the end of seven years the otter stopped coming and I went hungry again for three days, but then I was sent half a cake of flour and a slice of fish. My cup of whey fell into the sea and another one appeared to replace it, and it was full of good ale.'

'How –?' Germane began, but the old man interrupted him.

'You will see,' he said. 'The same food comes every day. I've lived here praying and doing penance all this time and I have never since gone hungry. Not only that, but it never rains nor snows nor becomes too hot on this rock, and there are never any storms.'

That was the end of the old man's story and, as he promised, food came that evening, enough for all of them, and in the curragh they found a vessel of good ale.

The next morning he spoke again.

'You will all reach your own country in safety. And Maildún will find an island on the way; on that island is the man who killed your father. But you are not to take your revenge, or harm him in any way. God has delivered you from all your dangers, in spite of your many faults and sins, and in the same way you must forgive your enemies for the things which they have done against you.'

Maildún thanked the old man and they took their leave and sailed away from the tiny rock.

Before long they came to a beautiful green island which had herds of cattle and sheep grazing all over the hills and valleys. They landed and searched for people but the island was empty except for the animals. There were no houses nor signs of buildings.

'We'll rest here for a while,' Maildún said. 'There is plenty of food for us.'

They stayed there for some time, killing a sheep or a cow when they were hungry. They regained their strength – and their land legs – and Germane slowly forgot about all the salmon he had had to eat.

One day two of the men were standing on top of a small hill and they saw a large falcon flying past.

'That's an Irish falcon,' one of them shouted, and Maildún heard him and came rushing up the hill.

'Watch the direction he takes,' Maildún said.

They stood together, their eyes shielded from the glare, and watched the sky.

'The south-east,' one of them said.

'Wait and see if he turns,' Maildún said.

But the falcon flew a straight course, true and unwavering and directly to the south-east.

They boarded the curragh at once, threw in all their possessions and what was left of the meat, and sailed to the south-east after the falcon. They rowed without stopping for a full day and then they sighted land in the evening dusk and it seemed to Maildún that it was like Erin.

It wasn't Erin but the small island which they had seen at the very beginning of their voyage – the island where they had heard a man boast that he had killed Maildún's father.

They landed on the shore and went up to the house and, as they approached, they realised that the people who lived there were at their evening meal.

Maildún motioned his men to keep quiet and they stood near the wall of the house and listened.

'It's as well Maildún can't see us now,' they heard a man say.

'He's dead,' another one said, 'drowned long ago in the storm.'

'But you'll never be sure,' the first one said, 'when you might feel his hand tapping you on the shoulder, waking you from your sleep.'

They heard a sigh, as though someone shivered.

'If he came now – this very minute,' someone said, 'what would we do?'

The head of the house spoke then – Maildún knew his voice.

'If Maildún should come now, out of the sea, having survived all that hardship, then I should welcome him and give him kindness, and forget that we were enemies.'

Maildún didn't wait to hear any more. He knocked at the door and told the doorkeeper who he was.

'I am here,' he said, 'safe and well after all my adventures.'

The chief of the household ordered the doors to be opened and then he went himself to bring in Maildún and his companions. They were given a great welcome by the whole household. Fresh clothes were brought and they sat down to a huge feast and ate and drank and talked until the dawn began to break.

They told the household about all the things they had seen and how God had shown them all his wonders and kept them safe. Everyone agreed that their story must never be forgotten and they stayed on the island for a few days, in an atmosphere of feasting and forgot all their quarrels.

They sailed, eventually, for Ireland and found it without difficulty. The curragh landed with a gentle swish on the shore they had left so long ago, and the men set out with a great shout of delight.

Maildún thanked them with tears in his eyes, and then told them to go home to their families, as he was going to do. They scattered the length and breadth of Ireland in search of their loved ones, but Diuran Lekerd took the piece of silver he had cut from the huge net at the Silver Pillar and laid it, according to his promise, at the high altar of Armagh.

6

Fionn and the Son of the King of Alba

Fionn was out hunting – one of his favourite sports – with his dog Bran on one of those special days when the hills were alive and his spear ran fast and true; before long he had so much game that he knew he couldn't carry it all home alone and he began to wish that he had brought Diarmuid or Mac Reithe with him. Suddenly he saw a man running towards him. The man had a long rope wound round and round his body and half-covering it; he was so tall that Fionn could see the whole world between his legs and the man's head and shoulders filled the sky.

He came up to Fionn and saluted him and Fionn asked him pleasantly where he was going.

'I am looking for a master,' the man said.

'And I,' Fionn said, 'am in need of a man to carry home my game. Will you do it for me?'

The man unwound the rope from his body. 'Whatever this rope can tie up, I can carry,' he said.

He put all the game into the rope and secured it into a big bundle and lifted it easily.

'Where shall I bring it?' he asked, and Fionn went ahead of him to show him the way to the castle.

Fionn ran as fast as he could but the man carrying the game kept up with him without difficulty; the castle sentry, seeing the man running far in the distance, steeped inside to warn the guard inside the gate.

'There's a man coming with a load as big as a mountain on his back,' he said, and went out again to find the huge man already at the gate. He dropped the bundle on the grass and it shook the castle to the very foundations.

'He might be useful,' Conán Maol said, the next day when Fionn sent the giant out to herd the cows, 'but he's strong enough to destroy us all.'

Fionn had reservations too; he was afraid permanent damage had been done to the castle when the game was dropped; even the man's bulk was frightening.

'Have him put to death,' Conán Maol said.

'But he's a good man,' Fionn said. 'How could I do that?'

'Send him to sow corn on the edge of the serpent's lake. The serpent will get rid of him – he swallows everybody who goes past – and no one can put the blame on you.'

Fionn thought about it, and then slept on it. He knew that Conán Maol was right – but it was always hard to take advice from Conán. The next morning he sent for the giant, gave him seven bullocks and a plough and a sack of grain and sent him to the serpent's lake in the north of Erin to sow corn.

The man went off amiably enough and began to plough as he had been directed. He managed to draw one furrow before the lake began to boil and the serpent leaped out into the field.

Within minutes it had swallowed the seven bullocks and was well into the plough, but the man grabbed the handle just as it was going down the serpent's throat; he pulled until the plough and six of the bullocks came free. The seventh bullock was lost in the belly of the serpent but, in spite of having retained a morsel of food, the creature went for the giant in a mad rage and they fought for seven days and seven nights. At the end of that time the serpent was as docile as a kitten and the man drove him back to the castle with the six bullocks.

The sentry, who had scarcely recovered from the sight of the giant with his bundle of game the previous week, ran for help when he saw the man coming back.

He has the size of a mountain before him,' he cried, and Conán Maol rushed out to look.

'Tell him to tie the serpent to that oak tree,' he said, 'quickly!' The sentry didn't have to be told twice; without fuss the serpent was tied to the tree and the man came and sat down to a good supper. The next morning he was back at his job of herding cows.

'Get rid of him,' Conán Maol said. 'He'll destroy us all.'

'How can I do that?' Fionn asked again. He had a few qualms of conscience about the serpent: the giant hadn't deserved that.

'There's a bullock in the north,' Conán said, 'and he drives a cloud of fog out of himself for seven days, then takes seven more days to draw it in again. Tomorrow's the last day for drawing in and if anyone comes near him he'll be swallowed alive.'

Fionn brought up the subject at supper time when the cowherd came back to the castle.

'I'm going to have a feast,' he said, and then hesitated, until a kick from Conán Maol made him go on. 'I need fresh beef,' he said, clearing his throat. 'I'd like you to go and get the bullock in the valley near the lake where you found the serpent.' He paused. 'I won't be ungrateful,' he said.

'I'll go first thing after breakfast tomorrow,' the man said.

He did as he had promised and when he came to the valley the bullock was asleep and drawing the last of the fog and the man found himself being drawn in with it. He grabbed an oak tree and held on to it for dear life but the bullock woke up and saw him; he let out a roar of rage and butted the giant seven miles over the top of the wood. The bullock was on him again before he had time to get up; he got another pitch from the horns which sent him back to the valley and broke three ribs in the process.

'This won't do,' the man said, and pulled up an oak tree to use as a club. He faced the bullock and they fought each other for five days and five nights until the bullock was as tame as a kitten and the man was able to drive him home to Fionn's castle.

The sentry saw them coming for miles and was in the gate to tell Conán Maol immediately.

'Tell the giant to tie the bullock to an oak tree. We don't want him in here,' Conán Maol said.

The cowherd tied the bullock to the oak, as he had been told, and advised Fionn to send for four of the best butchers in Erin to kill it with an axe, but when the butchers came and struck it, one after the other, none of them could fell it.

'Give it to me,' the giant said, and felled the bullock with one blow. The butchers moved in to skin the bullock but the man didn't like the way they did it, so he took his sword and had the job three-quarters done while they were still struggling with one leg.

The next morning the cowherd once again went out to his cows and Conán Maol could hardly wait until he'd gone before he went in search of Fionn.

'Now do you believe me?' he said. 'That man will kill us all, you and me and all the Fianna of Erin.'

'How can I put an end to a man like that?' Fionn asked. 'I have tried –'

'There's a wild sow in the north,' Conán said, 'and she has two big pigs of her own and all three have bags of poison in their tails. When they see any man they run and shake the poison over him. The smallest drop will kill.'

'We can try it,' Fionn said, not too hopefully. By now he realised that they would have to get rid of the giant but he realised too that it would not be easy.

'Well if he gets away from the sow and the pigs,' Conán said, 'there's the wild fox-man called Gruagach. He has one eye in the middle of his forehead and he carries a club that weighs a ton. One welt of that –'

Once again, Fionn called the cowherd after breakfast.

'I'm going to have a feast,' he said, 'and I'd like some fresh pork. There's a wild sow and two pigs in the north and if you get them for me I won't be ungrateful.'

'I'll go straight away,' the man said.

He left immediately, taking his sword with him, and found the wild sow and her pigs grazing in the place that Fionn had described. He crept up to them and cut the tails off the three of them before they even saw him; then he had to face the angry sow. He fought the sow for four days and five nights and killed her on the morning of the fifth day but, with the last blow the sword struck her in her backbone and he couldn't get it out. He had to break the blade to get it free and then he tore the sow down the middle with his bare hands, splitting her from head to tail by tearing her jaws apart.

He threw half the sow on his back but, at that moment, the one-eyed Gruagach came at him with his club. The cowherd jumped aside, caught the Gruagach by one leg as he came past, threw him up on to his shoulder on top of the half-sow, threw the other half of the sow on top of that and ran back to Fionn's castle as fast as he could.

The sentry heard the pounding of feet even before he saw him and he ran inside and said that the giant was back with another load like a mountain on his back.

'Go out and stop him before he gets here,' Conán Maol said, 'or he'll shake the –'

But before the sentry could get out again the giant was at the gate; his load was on the ground and the castle shook until every plate and dish inside it was broken.

The Gruagach got up from the mangled remains of the sow. Every bit of him was battered and bruised but he took to his heels and ran as fast and as far as he could from the giant and the castle, until he was safe in the north of Erin again.

The next day the giant was back herding the cows on Fionn's land. In the evening Oscar, the strongest of the Fianna, came up to him as he was munching on the thigh bone of a bullock and grabbed one end of the bone. They pulled and pulled until the bone broke in half and then they started quarrelling as to who should keep the biggest half.

'I'll keep mine,' Oscar said, 'and that is for you.' He hit the cowherd a sharp slap across the head.

The Fianna held their breath but the cowherd didn't return the blow. He ignored Oscar and went back to his bone, but the next morning he went to Fionn and asked for his wages.

'Gladly,' Fionn said, delighted that he was leaving. 'You are the best cowherd I ever had,' and he paid him on the spot.

'I am not a cowherd,' the giant said. 'I'm the son of the king of Alba and I'd like to invite you and all the Fianna to my castle in

Cahirciveen in Kerry. I'll give you a great feast and my people will welcome you.'

The castle proved to be the finest that the Fianna had ever seen. Each room boasted three fires and each fire had seven spits but, when the Fianna went to sit down, they found that there was only one fire in each room.

'Get up!' Fionn yelled. 'This is an enchanted place!'

They tried to get up but they were stuck to their seats and when they tried to move the seats they found that they were stuck to the floor. And then the last fire went out and they were in darkness.

'You'll have to chew your thumb,' Conán Maol said to Fionn, 'to get us out of this.'

Fionn stuck his thumb in his mouth as he had done years ago when he tasted the Salmon of Knowledge, and knew immediately the danger they were in; then he put both hands to his mouth and blew his special whistle and up in the north of Erin his two sons heard him. One was fishing and the other hurling but when they heard Fionn's whistle they knew that he was in trouble and the Fianna with him.

They set off straight away in the direction of the sound and didn't stop until they reached the door of the enchanted castle. They knocked and Fionn called out to know who they were.

'Your two sons,' they said.

'We are in great trouble,' Fionn said. 'The cowherd was no cowherd at all, but the son of the king of Alba and he wants my head before he has eaten three more meals. His army is on the way here, and he has cut off our escape by the ford.'

'Leave it to us,' Fionn's sons said. They went into the night and met the king of Alba's army at the ford.

'Let us pass,' the son of the king of Alba said, recognising them.

'We will not,' they said, and began to fight. They killed every last man of the army except the son of the king of Alba and then they went back to their father to report.

'There is more danger,' Fionn said, sucking his thumb. 'An old woman will come and touch the lips of all the dead men with something from a little pot, and they'll all come back to life. And before that you'll hear music at the ford, and the music will put you to sleep.'

'What shall we do?' asked Fionn's sons.

'You must kill the old hag,' Fionn said.

The two young men went back to the ford and before long they began to fall asleep from the music.

'Kick my foot,' one said to the other. They kicked each other until they were black and blue but it was no use; then they each took a spear and drove it through the foot of the other but, in spite of this, they both fell asleep.

The old woman went around the dead army with her little pot, touching the lips of the soldiers and bringing them back to life but, when she crossed the ford at the head of the army, she fell over the sleeping brothers and spilled what was left in the pot over them.

They jumped up, well and strong, and killed the army of the king of Alba with two huge stones from the ford; then they killed the old woman and left her there and went to knock at the door of the castle.

'Who is it?' Fionn called.

'Your two sons,' they said. 'We have done everything you said.'

'There's one more thing to do,' Fionn said, 'to set us free. You must go to the three kings in the north and from each of them take a silver goblet. They are having a feast today and you will have to cut off their heads and fill the goblets with their blood to release us.'

'And bring the goblets here?' they asked.

'Yes,' Fionn said. 'Rub the blood on the keyhole of this door and it will open, and then rub the seats with blood and we will be able to get up.'

His sons went to the north of Erin and brought back the goblets and, as Fionn said, when a little blood was rubbed onto the keyhole the door flew open and light filled the room. The brothers rubbed blood on all the seats and the Fianna got up stiffly and stretched themselves. Conán Maol was the only one who did not have a seat. He was sitting on the floor with his back to the wall and when they came to him all the blood was gone. The Fianna hurried past him, anxious to escape and not too worried about his fate. Conán Maol never had a good word for anyone and he had got them into more trouble over the years than all the giants and enchanted castles in the country.

Conán caught hold of Diarmuid as he went past. 'If it was a woman sitting here you wouldn't leave her,' he said.

Diarmuid turned and tried to pull him free; then Goll took Conán's other hand and they pulled and pulled and tore him from the wall. When he came free all the skin from his head to his heels was left on the floor and wall behind him and, on the way home, they killed a sheep for food and clapped the skin on to Conán's back. It grew into his body and he became well and so strong that they sheared him every year and had enough wool to make clothes for the Fianna for ever after.

7

The Magic Cloak

Fionn was drinking one night with some of the Fianna, Diarmuid, Mac Reithe, Oisín and Oscar among them; against their better judgement they had brought their wives for company; they had also brought Conán Maol and a couple of servants.

The evening began pleasantly enough. Conán Maol, for once, managed not to say anything out of the way, and the wives made themselves agreeable: they were only too pleased not to be left at home while the Fianna indulged in their usual pursuits.

'Make sure there's no mention of a fishing line or a wild boar or we'll be left sitting here,' Oscar's wife whispered to Oisín's.

'Or an enchanted castle,' Oisín's wife whispered back, and they both laughed.

'What's amusing you?' Fionn asked.

'Nothing,' the two women said, and held their sides with mirth.

'We've given you too much to drink,' Fionn said, disgusted.

'You should be glad to have us,' Diarmuid's wife said. 'Six women like us, pure and faithful …'

'Most women are pure and faithful,' Fionn said, unimpressed. 'And in any case the world is full of sin.'

'If that was meant to be praise,' Oscar's wife said, raising her voice, 'then I don't think much of it.'

'It was not meant to be praise,' Fionn said, and then added hastily, as the light of battle glinted in the women's eyes, 'nor do I mean to say anything against you – merely that there's nothing especially praiseworthy about being pure. We expect it of our wives.'

'Oh do you?' Fionn's wife, Maignes, said.

'And we expect it of our husbands, a gentle voice said behind her, but no one was sure who had spoken.

'There are many women,' Fionn said, ignoring the danger signals, 'who have slept with one husband only.'

None of the wives were in the mood to argue this point. They drew away from their husbands and stood together in a little group whispering.

'We should be able to prove it,' Mac Reithe's wife said, and the others nodded and frowned.

'I can show you how to prove it,' a clear voice said, and they turned to see a strange woman standing nearby. She had been watching them and listening to their conversation.

'If you could really do that ...' Maignes said. She paused. 'How could you do it?'

They had seen her cloak. It was too beautiful to ignore, made of lovely golden threads and covering her to the ground. The Fianna had seen it too, and heard what she had to say. They moved in closer to look at it.

'This cloak will test you,' she said. She undid the fastening and slipped out of it.

'How?' Maignes said again.

'If a woman puts it on it will only cover her if she is truly virtuous and faithful to one man only.'

She held out the cloak invitingly and there was a silence for a moment while the wives considered the situation. The woman smiled mockingly and waved the cloak in front of the Fianna. The Fianna didn't move – they were considering the situation too – but Conán Maol, always ready to rush in first and think afterwards, asked the woman to give it to his wife.

His wife took it, reluctantly.

'Put it on,' Conán Maol said.

She put it on slowly, fumbling with the fastening, and the lovely smooth gold garment wrinkled up and shrank to almost nothing. Before the Fianna could take breath, Conán had raised his spear and killed his wife on the spot.

The woman undid the cloak from the dead woman and handed it to Diarmuid's wife. Diarmuid smiled complacently. Everyone knew that his wife was an excellent woman, and quite faultless. She took the cloak but she did not smile back at her husband as she put it around her shoulders. The cloak scarcely covered her breasts and she threw it away from her; Diarmuid pushed his way out of the room, knocking drinking vessels to the ground as he went.

'You,' the strange woman said to Oscar's wife. 'You from far away. You try it.'

Oscar took the precaution of turning away before the rest of the Fianna saw that the cloak didn't reach to his wife's waist.

There was a marked lack of enthusiasm about the remaining wives. No one, it seemed, was quite so anxious to prove her virtue as she had been.

Oisín's took it next.

'What a shame – it doesn't fit her,' Diarmuid's wife said.

'What about your wife?' the woman said to Fionn.

'No!' Maignes said.

'Oh yes you will,' Fionn said, striding forward. 'If the others try it, then so must you.'

Maignes turned her back on him but Fionn pulled her round and gave her the cloak. It shrivelled up around her ears and they faced each other expressionlessly for a moment before Fionn took the cloak from her.

He held it in his hands for a moment, and then Mac Reithe asked for it.

'I'd like to see if my wife is the same,' he said.

The golden folds slid effortlessly around his wife's body. No one spoke and Mac Reithe's wife looked down modestly. The cloak covered her from neck to feet.

'But her toe is sticking out,' Maignes said, maliciously.

The colour came up to Mac Reithe's wife's face.

'That was the kiss I gave to Diarmuid,' she said, annoyed, 'but I didn't mean it –'

Maignes laughed, and Mac Reithe's wife threw the cloak at her.

'You can say anything about me, but there's plenty I can say about the rest of you!' She rushed out of the room and Fionn snatched the cloak from his wife and thrust it at the strange woman.

'Get out,' he said, 'and take your wretched cloak with you.' The woman stood still, the mocking smile still on her face. 'Out!' Fionn yelled, 'before you do any more damage.' He gripped her arm and dragged her to the door. 'And don't ever come back,' he said, as he slammed the door after her.

It was a long time before the Fianna took their wives drinking with them again – even longer before they took Conán Maol.

8

Oisín in Tír-na-nÓg

The king of Tír-na-nÓg had ruled for along time, holding his throne against the challengers who came every seven years, by law, to race against him. The race was run from the front of the royal palace to the top of a hill two miles away, and on top of that hill was a chair. The new king was the man who ran fast enough to sit in the chair first and, for many years, the same man had won the race and been re-elected.

As time went by, though, far from becoming a complacent winner, the king became more and more afraid that one day he simply would not run fast enough. He called his druid for advice.

'You'll keep your crown forever,' the druid said, reassuringly, 'unless your son-in-law takes it from you.'

The king had only one child – a daughter – and so far she was unwed, but she was very beautiful with long golden hair and clear blue eyes and a skin more fair than had ever been seen even in that land of youth. She had no equal in Erin nor in any country of the world. It was clear to her father that she would have no difficulty in finding a brave and noble husband – and one, moreover, who would easily outrun his father-in-law. The king told the druid to cast a spell on the Princess Niamh so that she would never marry, but the princess was known and loved throughout all Tír-na-nÓg, and the druid refused.

'Then give me your rods,' the king said, angrily, and took them from the druid before he could gather them up and hide them. The king then called the princess and struck her with one of the magic rods and changed her beautiful head into that of a pig.

'No one will marry her now,' the king said to the druid, and sent Niamh back to her own quarters where she was only too glad to remain out of sight.

The druid was full of remorse. He went to see the princess and told her how sorry he was.

'Must I be like this forever?' the princess asked, tears running down her pink, hairy snout.

The druid thought hard. 'There is only one cure,' he said. 'You must marry a mortal – not any mortal, but a son of Fionn Mac Cumhaill of Erin – and then you will get back your own shape.'

When Niamh heard this she could not wait to leave Tír-na-nÓg and travel to Erin. She went first to Knock an Áir where the Fianna were then living and bided her time until she could meet the sons of Fionn Mac Cumhaill. She watched the young men while they were out hunting and fishing and she picked out Oisín, the poet, and liked what she saw. He was tall and strong and handsome but he was gentle too. Niamh watched him as he stood and looked at the sun lighting misty valleys, and watched him too as he freed a frightened doe from a thicket and sent it on its way. There and then she fell in love with him.

Niamh made it her business to get to know Oisín. She was always in the hills when he went hunting and, each day when he was fishing, he found her sitting quietly on the river bank. She was there when he needed company, silent when he was thoughtful and full of laughter when he was gay, and she did everything to make life easy for him.

One day Oisín was out with his men and his father's three dogs.

He had wandered far away into the hills around Killarney and had taken so much game that his men were too tired to carry it. They went home and left him to manage it himself.

The princess had followed the hunt closely all day and when the men left Oisín on his own she came to him to help him.

'I don't want to leave any of it behind,' Oisín said, looking at the big pile of game.

'Tie some up in a bundle for me to carry,' she said, 'to lighten your load.'

Oisín tied a small bundle for her and took the rest himself and they started back to the castle. It was a warm evening and the air was heavy. After a while they stopped to rest; they threw down the game and put their backs to a cool stone at the side of the road. The princess was hot and out of breath and she opened the neck of her dress to try to cool herself.

Oisín looked at her sideways and then his eyes fell to her lovely round breasts and white shoulders.

'It's a pity you have a pig's head,' he said, 'because I've never seen such a beautiful body before.'

'I didn't always have a pig's head,' the princess said. 'My father put a spell on me so that I could never marry. He stole the druid's wand and struck me with it ...' The princess paused. 'There is a cure,' she added.

'Then we must find it,' Oisín said.

'I have already found it,' the princess said. 'The druid told me that I should marry one of the sons of Fionn Mac Cumhaill and then I would have my own face back again.' She paused, delicately. 'And so I came to Erin and I found you.'

'If that's all that's keeping the pig's head,' Oisín said, 'we'll get rid of it straight away.'

The princess smiled at him – as well as she could in her situation – and held out her hand, and they were married on the spot, without formality – without even picking up the game to take it home. Immediately the princess was transformed and Oisín was speechless when he saw how beautiful she was. A slender golden diadem encircled her head and, instead of the heavy grey homespun dress which she had been wearing, she was now dressed in a brown silk robe, fastened with a golden brooch and spangled with red-gold stars. It fell in smooth soft folds to the ground and her yellow hair cascaded down it almost to her waist. In her small white hand she held the bridle of a snow-white horse. The horse had shoes of pure yellow gold and a golden bit in his mouth, and he was the most handsome horse Oisín had ever seen.

'My name is Niamh of the Golden Hair,' she said, as he gazed at her.

'Come home with me,' he said, at last, 'and meet my father and the Fianna.'

'I must go back to Tír-na-nÓg,' she said, and the horse neighed and pawed the ground. 'Come with me – or we will never see each other again.'

'With you?' Oisín said. 'To Tír-na-nÓg?'

'You are my husband now,' Niamh said. She smiled at him. 'There are jewels there, and gold and silver and honey and wine; the trees bear fruit and flowers and green leaves all the year round, and you will have a hundred swords and a hundred robes of silk and satin and a hundred steeds like this one, and a hundred hounds, and herds of cows and sheep without number.' She paused for breath. 'And a coat of mail that cannot be pierced and a sword which never missed a stroke, and a hundred warriors to wait on you. And we will be forever young and live together as man and wife.' Niamh paused again and added, woman-like, 'and as well as that, I put you under a solemn *geasa* to come with me.'

Oisín looked around him at the blue and purple hills and the shimmering lake, and he thought of his father and his companions of the Fianna and then he looked at the golden-haired Niamh beside him and he was lost.

He helped her to mount the white horse and jumped up behind her and they travelled through Kerry, over the mountains and across the valleys, never stopping and never looking backwards, until they left the land and stepped into the sea. They rode across the waves, barely touching the sun-dazzled water; they passed through rainbows and sunshine and saw shimmering mansions and tall pinnacles of castles as they went, and green lawns and brilliant flowers and cities of marble and gold, and then they came at last to a silver strand and rode up a clover-covered bank under giant beech trees. Birds sang and bees hummed and all the people of Tír-na-nÓg came out to welcome him to their shining land.

The king had had a long time to be sorry for what he had done to his daughter. He had been sure that he had lost her forever and, when he heard that she was coming home, even though she was bringing home a mortal husband with her, he gave orders that a feast was to be prepared, and he welcomed the couple with outstretched arms. They celebrated far into the night and during the following months Oisín lived very happily with his lovely young bride. It was beautiful country and had everything that Niamh had described; the people were gay and contented; Niamh was gentle and loving and Oisín lived the life of a king.

Before long he was king indeed. During the following year the time came for the race to be run from the castle to the chair on the hill to decide the next ruler. All the nobility assembled at the castle and Oisín joined the race with them. He ran faster than anyone and was in the chair before any of the other champions had run even half way. He was appointed king that day and, from then on, ruled the country firmly and fairly and no one ever challenged him to run to the chair again.

But Oisín often thought of Erin and his friends and of the salmon leaping and the mayfly drowsy in the sun on the dappled water, and the stag running fleet of foot across the mountains.

'I wish I could see my father and my friends again,' he said, one day when Niamh found him staring sadly at the hills around the castle.

'Are you not happy here?' she asked.

'Yes, I'm happy,' Oisín said, 'but three years is a long time, and I would like to see them.'

'It is even more than three years,' Niamh said. 'This is the Land of the Ever Young.'

'It does not seem any more than three,' Oisín said.

'It is three hundred,' Niamh said. 'Everything will be changed in Erin.'

But Oisín did not believe her. As the days went by he pined more and more for his own people and Niamh watched him and grew sad.

'If you must go,' she said, eventually, 'I'll give you this white horse to take you back, but you must stay on it and not dismount. If your foot touches the ground of Erin, the horse will fly back here without you and you will become an old man, and –' she sighed, 'and we will never see each other again.'

'Just one day,' Oisín promised. 'If I can just see my father and my friends then I'll come straight back to you –' He held her close.

'And you will be satisfied?' Niamh asked.

'With you, yes,' Oisín said. He moved back so that she could see his face, and he smiled at her.

Niamh prepared the white horse and gave him exact instructions.

'And be sure to stay on its back,' she said again to Oisín. 'The horse will carry you safely there and back, so long as you do as I say.'

Oisín rode day and night without stopping. He could not wait to see his homeland again. He travelled back across the hills and valleys with mounting excitement, looking for familiar landmarks but, although he had come at last to Erin, everything was changed. His father's castle was a mouldering ruin, forests had been but down and others had grown elsewhere; the rivers still ran with salmon and the hills were alive with game but the people were not the tall proud hunters of the Fianna: they were small and stunted and eked out a miserable existence scratching at the land.

'Perhaps I've been spoiled in Tír-na-nÓg,' Oisín said, to himself, 'but I don't remember anything like this.'

He came to Knock Patrick in Munster where he found a herdsman working in a field of cows. In the field was a huge flat stone.

'Will you turn the stone over for me?' Oisín asked the man.

'I will not,' the herdsman said. 'Twenty men couldn't lift that stone.'

Oisín rode nearer and reached down and, remembering Niamh's warning, he held firmly on to his mount. He flicked over the stone with his hand and underneath he saw the ridged and curved horn of the Fianna. It was shaped like a sea-shell and, when anyone of the Fianna blew it, the rest would come to him wherever they might be.

'Will you give me the horn?' Oisín said to the herdsman.

'I will not,' the man said. 'A dozen men could not lift it from the ground.'

Oisín reached down even further – above all he wanted to call the Fianna to him – and stretched out his arm for the horn. He slipped and put one foot to the ground to save himself and, in that instant, the horse vanished and Oisín was thrown into the field; he lay there, blind and helpless and old, at the feet of the herdsman.

St Patrick was living nearby and the herdsman went to him for help and the saint sent a man and a horse to bring Oisín to his house. The saint also found a serving boy to care for the old man, and a cook to feed him. He told the cook to be sure to give Oisín bread and beef and butter every day.

Oisín lived there for a while, being cared for by the servants. He talked each day with St Patrick, telling him about the old days with Fionn Mac Cumhaill and Oscar and Goll. And of Conán Maol of the foolish tongue, and Diarmuid and the love-spot, and of their fights and their feasts and their hunting, and how they freed themselves from druidic spells and rescued maidens in distress.

St Patrick was busy at that time putting up an enormous building. His men worked hard during the day building walls but each night everything was levelled again by unknown hands. St Patrick told Oisín of his problems and Oisín sighed and said that if he wasn't such a weary old man he would put a stop to the forces who were destroying the building.

'Could you do that?' St Patrick asked, 'if you had your strength again?'

'I could,' Oisín said. Even at the thought his voice became stronger.

St Patrick prayed very hard for Oisín and his prayers were answered. The blind old man regained his sight and his vigour. He went to the woods and cut a huge club and that night he stood proudly on guard over St Patrick's new building.

During the night an enormous roar shattered the stillness and a huge bull charged up to the building and began to uproot the foundations and fling down the pillars.

Oisín faced him and they fought a hot and terrible battle. The bull was strong and had a druid's powers but Oisín was stronger and eventually he gained the upper hand. He left the bull dead in front of the building and then stretched himself out and took a well-earned rest.

St Patrick was waiting at home for news and when daylight came and he had heard nothing he sent a messenger to find out what had happened. The messenger found the ground torn up and all the signs of a desperate battle and then he found the bull lying dead; finally he found Oisín lying on the ground fast asleep. He went back to report.

'So he killed the monster,' St Patrick said. And he could easily kill the rest of us if he had a mind, he thought to himself.

St Patrick prudently took away Oisín's strength while he slept and he woke to find himself once again a blind old man. The cook and the servant boy continued to look after him and St Patrick talked with him every day and listened to the stories of Fionn and the Fianna.

St Patrick was looking for a patron to support his house. He had a neighbour, a Jew, who had the finest haggard of corn in Erin. The Jew and St Patrick became very friendly and before long the Jew told the saint that he could have as much corn for his house as one man could thrash from the haggard in one day.

St Patrick went home and told Oisín about the offer.

'If I had my sight and strength,' Oisín said, 'I'd thrash as much corn in one day as would do your whole house for a year.'

'Would you do that for me?' St Patrick said.

'I would,' Oisín said, and St Patrick prayed again long and hard, and strength and sight came back to Oisín.

He went to the woods at daybreak and pulled up two ashes and made a flail of them and then, after breakfast, he went to the Jew's haggard. He slashed the first stack of wheat with his ash sticks and broke the stack in two. Then he went around the haggard and thrashed the rest of the corn.

The Jew ran backwards and forwards in dismay as Oisín systematically cleared out his precious store. There was nothing the Jew could do to stop him and when Oisín went back to St Patrick and told him to send his men to collect the wheat, he left the Jew staring at his empty haggard and tearing out his hair in clumps.

St Patrick looked at the triumphant Oisín nervously. This man, he thought, had a face like thunder and the resources of an army and, when he heard what Oisín had done in the haggard in one day, he promptly knocked the strength out of him again.

The men went to collect the wheat and there was twice as much there as they could carry and twice as much as they needed.

The Jew recovered slowly from the shock and Oisín settled

down in St Patrick's house again, being cared for by the cook and the serving boy.

The food, however, was less plentiful and Oisín became angry with the cook. He complained to St Patrick who called the cook to his room and, in front of Oisín, asked her what she was giving the old man to eat.

The cook drew herself up. 'At every meal,' she said, 'he gets the bread I bake on the large griddle, and he gets all the butter from one churn, and a quarter of the beef as well.'

'There's nothing wrong with that,' St Patrick said to Oisín. 'Isn't that enough for you?'

'I've seen many a blackbird with legs bigger than the quarter of beef you give me,' Oisín said to the cook, 'and I've seen many an ivy leaf bigger than your so called large griddle that you bake my bread on, and I've seen many a rowan berry bigger than the bit of butter I get.'

'That's a lie!' the cook screamed, but Oisín turned away and didn't answer. He was thinking of the huge feasts he used to have, long, long ago with the Fianna.

The next day he began to plan to go hunting again.

'Bring me the pick of the hound's litter,' he said to the serving boy and the boy came back and said there were three whelps and he didn't know which to choose.

An ox had been slaughtered the day before and Oisín told the boy to bring the hide and hang it up. 'And throw the pups against the hide,' he said, 'one after the other.'

The first two fell on the ground but the third whelp clung to the hide and held on for all he was worth.

'Keep that one and drown the others,' Oisín said, when the boy told him how the pups had behaved. 'And feed the mother well too,' he said.

Oisín had completed the first part of his plan, but he had to wait another year and a day before the dog was old enough to go hunting. When that day came both dog and boy were as excited as he was.

'Put a chain around the dog,' Oisín said, and the three set out, the boy guiding the blind old man and the dog running happily beside them.

First they went to the place where Oisín had fallen from the white horse on his journey from Tír-na-nÓg.

'I lost everything here,' he said, touching the springy black earth, 'wife, country, father, friends –'

The boy touched his arm in sympathy and the dog nuzzled against his cloak.

'But we're not finished yet,' Oisín said. He felt around on the ground with his hands until he found the sea-shell shape of the horn of the Fianna and then he smiled and picked it up and put it under his cloak.

They went next to Thrush's Glen, and Oisín stood at the edge of it and began to sound the horn. Birds and animals came rushing towards them and Oisín blew and blew until the glen was full from end to end.

'What can you see?' Oisín said to the boy.

'Hundreds of animals and birds. The glen is full –'

'And what is the dog doing?'

'The hair is rising on his back,' the boy said, 'and he's watching the game.'

'Anything else?' Oisín asked.

'There's a huge black bird over there, to the north. It's settled in a tree.'

'Good,' Oisín said. 'Exactly what I wanted. Has the dog seen it?'

'He must have,' the boy said. 'His eyes are starting out of his head and every hair on his body is standing on end.'

'Then slip the chain!' Oisín said, and the boy let the dog go. It rushed through the glen killing everything in its path and when everything else was dead he turned on the blackbird and killed that too. And then he turned on his masters and came bounding towards them. Oisín heard him coming and he took a brass ball from his cloak and gave it to the boy.

'Throw this at the dog's mouth or he'll kill us,' he said.

The boy was shaking with fear. 'I can't,' he said.

'If you don't he'll tear us to pieces,' Oisín said, urgently.

The boy began to cry. 'I can't,' he said again.

'Then come behind me and guide my hand,' Oisín said, and the boy did as he was told and between them they threw the ball hard and true into the dog's mouth.

'What happened?' Oisín said, into the silence.

'The dog is dead,' the boy said. He had stopped crying.

'Good,' Oisín said. 'Now bring me over to the blackbird.'

'What about the rest of the game?' the boy said.

'I'm not interested in that,' Oisín said.

They found the bird and Oisín prepared it while the boy lit a fire. Oisín cooked it all except for one of the legs and then they had a feast the like of which Oisín hadn't enjoyed for years.

'There is nothing like a meal after the hunt,' the old man said to the boy, as they licked their fingers after the last morsel was gone.

The meat had been juicy and succulent and lightly flavoured with the smell of woodsmoke; Oisín had eaten and eaten until finally he was satisfied.

'Now,' he said, 'we'll go further into the woods.'

They walked on together and after a while Oisín asked the boy if he could see anything unusual.

'I see an ivy bush,' the boy said, 'with the largest leaves that I have ever seen.'

'Bring me one leaf,' Oisín said, and the boy went over and picked a leaf, and then he found a rowan berry and he picked that too, under Oisín's direction. And then they carried home the blackbird's leg, the huge ivy leaf and the rowan berry.

When they reached the house Oisín sent for the cook and talked to her in front of St Patrick.

Oisín pointed to the blackbird's leg. 'Which is larger,' he asked, 'the bird's leg or the quarter of beef you gave me yesterday?'

'The bird's leg,' the cook said, reluctantly.

'You were right,' St Patrick said to Oisín.

Oisín took out the ivy leaf. 'And is this not larger than the piece of bread you baked for me?'

The cook looked nervous and didn't answer.

'Come, come,' St Patrick said. 'Is it larger, or is it not?'

'It's larger than the bread and the griddle put together,' the cook said, her words tumbling out unevenly, 'but on my life I've never seen a leaf that size before –'

St Patrick turned to Oisín.

'You were right again,' he said.

Oisín took out the rowan berry. 'And is this larger than the churn of butter you say you gave to me?'

It wasn't – it was an ordinary berry – but the cook was in no state to notice that.

'It's larger than the churn and the butter put together,' she said.

'You were right every time,' murmured St Patrick.

Oisín had had a good day. He had overcome his feebleness and his blindness; he had been hunting with no more than a dog and a boy to help him; he had eaten meat which he had killed himself – and now he had put St Patrick in his place.

He raised his hand to complete the day's work, and cut the head off the cook with a sideways sweep of his palm.

'And you,' he said, triumphantly, 'will never call an honest man a liar again.'

9

THE CHASE OF SLIEVE CULLINN

One of the stories which Oisín recounted to St Patrick on his return from Tír-na-nÓg was the one which reminded him of his own plight: the day that Fionn Mac Cumhaill was turned instantly from a strong man in his prime into a feeble old man.

Fionn Mac Cumhaill had many admirers among the women of Ireland but the jealous love of Milucra very nearly brought about his downfall. Milucra and Aina were two beautiful sisters each determined to marry Fionn. They were the daughters of Culand, the smith of the Dé Dananns. The Dé Dananns, after their defeat by Milesius, had retreated to live underground in the remotest parts of the country and Milucra and Aina had their home in a fairy palace beneath Slieve Cullinn, a bleak mountain in Armagh.

Neither of the two sisters was in any way certain that she had the affection of Fionn. They walked together one evening near his palace on the flat-topped Hill Of Allen, talking of this and that, and then of men in a roundabout way and, eventually, of the kind of man they might marry, each unwilling to admit that it was one particular man who filled their thoughts.

Aina was more open that Milucra but even she would go no further than to say that she would never marry a man with grey hair, and Milucra listened and thought of Fionn's golden head and, like many women before and since, she made up her mind that if she couldn't have him, then neither would her sister.

Milucra went back immediately to Slieve Cullinn and called

on the Dé Dananns to help her. They came with their magical powers and at her bidding, made a lake near the top of the mountain. Milucra was very pleased. She gazed at its still waters and smiled and then breathed a druid's curse over it.

It was easy to lure Fionn to Slieve Cullinn. Milucra chose a bright morning and sent a leaping lively doe running from the bushes near the garden at Allen and Fionn, strolling on the lawn, couldn't resist the chase. He called his companions but they didn't hear him. The doe was running like the wind and Fionn couldn't wait. He set chase with only his two dogs, Bran and Sciolán, for protection. The doe turned northwards, just keeping ahead of the dogs, with Fionn hard on their heels. He was armed only with a sword and the Fianna were left far behind, unaware that he had gone. They travelled, the doe and the hounds and the solitary man, further and further northwards until they reached the mountain of Slieve Cullinn – and then Fionn lost the doe. He sent the dogs to search one side of the hill, while he searched the other, but they never caught sight of her again.

Fionn couldn't understand how they had lost the scent so easily. He whistled for his dogs and then waited and listened. He heard a cry nearby, whistled again, and then followed the sound. But it wasn't the dogs, nor any sound of the hunt that he'd heard, but the hopeless sound of someone weeping. He found a girl sitting at the edge of the lake and he caught his breath because he had never before seen anything so lovely. Her hair was heavy and golden like his own, but her skin was as white as the apple blossom, and her mouth as red as the magical quicken berries. The delicate pink of her cheeks was heightened by her weeping and, when she looked up at Fionn, her eyes sparkled like the stars in a frosty sky.

When she saw him she stopped crying for a moment and he asked her if she had seen his hounds.

'No,' said the girl, 'I haven't seen anything of the chase. I was sitting thinking only of my own troubles. I don't think I would have seen your hounds if they had passed next to me.' She began to cry again, as though her heart would break, and Fionn, forgetting immediately about his own problems, asked her what was the matter.

'Have you lost your husband, or has death taken a child from you? Tell me if there's anything I can do? I can't bear to see anyone in distress.'

The girl looked at him. 'You are one of the Fianna, are you not? And the Fianna are pledged to help all women in distress?'

Fionn admitted that he was.

'I had a gold ring on my finger,' she said, 'precious beyond price, and it has fallen off and rolled down the hill into the water. I watched it roll away and now it has gone out of sight.' The girl had quite stopped weeping now. She looked at Fionn with her bright pale eyes. 'If you are indeed of the Fianna, I put you under a solemn *geasa* that no hero would dare to break to search for my ring and not to stop searching until you find it.'

Fionn had not the slightest desire to swim in the dark waters of the lake; he had his hounds to find and the doe to pursue and it was a long journey back to his home on the Hill of Allen, but as the girl had said no true member of the Fianna could break a *geasa* and face his companions without shame again. A *geasa* was both a solemn vow and an enchantment, and so he had no choice but to plunge straight away into the water and search every part of the lake. He dived to the bottom and looked in every nook and cranny and swam around the lake three times before he at last found the ring. He swam over to the girl and handed it to her from the water.

She took it without a word of thanks and then dived into the water and disappeared from sight. Fionn, puzzled, pulled himself out of the lake but as soon as his feet touched dry land, he felt overcome with weakness. His legs and arms trembled and his skin withered up; he had become a shrivelled old man. He lay there, helpless, and in absolute misery, and eventually that was where his hounds found him. They came up to him and whined and sniffed but they didn't recognise him. He was a stranger and not their master at all. They left him and went sniffing and searching round and round the lake, running and howling and looking in vain for Fionn Mac Cumhaill.

It wasn't until the evening that the Fianna missed their leader. They were together in the banqueting hall in the palace of Allen, spread about in little groups; the hall was full of music and warm with talk and laughter. Fionn's nephew, Kylta Mac Ronán, missed him first. He looked about the great hall, his eyes going from the musicians to those still eating and then to the quiet chess players in the corner, and he stood up suddenly, in alarm, and asked if anyone had seen Fionn that day.

'I haven't seen him,' he said, 'nor is he here now.'

The evening was spoiled. The Fianna, realising that their leader had been missing for hours, and that no one knew where he had gone, stopped their music and their feasting straight away and made plans to go to look for him. Only Conán Maol was pleased.

'I hope you search for a year and do not find him,' he said. 'And if you don't then I will be your king in his stead.'

In spite of their anxiety, and due perhaps to the feasting, the Fianna couldn't help laughing at Conán Maol. He never missed an opportunity to promote his own interests. They left him brooding and went to ask the servants who had last seen Fionn, and learned that he had gone northwards in pursuit of a doe, with his two dogs. They gathered a strong party together, led by Kylta and Oisín, and went after him keeping close together and setting a fast pace without stopping to rest or slowing down until they reached the mountain of Slieve Cullinn.

They lost the track there and so they began to search the slopes, pushing through bushes and clambering over rough rocky places, until they came to the lake and found the grey-headed old man sitting at the water's edge. Oisín went up to him to ask if he had seen Fionn and the Fianna came and stood behind him in a group. Oisín wondered if he was a farmer, up from the valley to fish the lake, but when he saw how grey he was, and how his skin sagged and stretched in pouches over his sharp bones, he thought that he could not be any kind of fisherman, and that he looked not just old but worn away by sickness. When Oisín asked him if he had seen a noble-looking strong man pass by, with two hounds chasing a doe, the old man didn't answer. He didn't look at them. He let his head drop and his limbs shook all over; then he began to make small distressed sounds, putting his hands together and rubbing them anxiously. They were gentle with him for a while, hoping that he might have something to tell them, but he said nothing, just went on moaning and shaking and wringing his hands together.

The Fianna became irritated then and drew their swords and threatened him with instant death if he didn't tell them straight away where their chief was. They felt sure that he had seen them, but even the threat of death didn't move the old man. He stayed crouched up on the bank of the lake, a picture of abject misery, unable or unwilling to speak a word.

The Fianna were at a loss as to where to search next and finally they decided to go back down the mountain. When the old man saw that they were going to leave he lifted his head and beckoned Kylta Mac Ronán. Kylta went over to him and the old man whispered the truth in his ear: that he was Fionn Mac Cumhaill, their king, reduced to this sorry state by enchantment.

Kylta, appalled, told the others what had happened and they set up a horrified shout of anger and misery. They shouted again and again and made so much noise that foxes and badgers ran terrified from their dens on the mountain. Conán Maol, however, was pleased at this turn of events. He stepped forward, straddling the ground in front of the withered old man, and drew his sword and brandished it in front of him; and then he began to insult Fionn and the Fianna in the foulest language he could think of.

'And I am going to kill you, Fionn Mac Cumhaill,' he shouted. 'I'm going to strike off your head! You never gave me any credit for anything I did for you, or praised me after I did battle for you. You've never forgotten that it was my clanspeople who killed your father, and you have begrudged my existence ever since. It gives me enormous pleasure to see you reduced to this. I only wish the rest of your clan were there with you! I'd make short work of you all and afterwards I'd have the greatest enjoyment in building a cairn to their memory!'

Only Oscar took any notice of him. The Fianna were used to these sudden outbursts. Oscar looked at him scornfully and told him it was not worth the trouble of drawing a sword to teach him a lesson.

'But if we hadn't so much to think about at the moment, I

would most certainly smash your foul mouth with my fist!'

'Actions speak louder than words,' Conán said, loftily, 'and it was the actions of my people, the Clann Mórna, who gave the Fianna their reputation for bravery, not the chicken-livered Clann Baskin.'

This was too much for Oscar. He rushed at Conán, intent on murder, and Conán, realising that he'd gone too far, fled behind the protective shields of the Fianna and begged them to save him. It took several of the warriors to hold Oscar back and quite a bit of time to soothe him down. Eventually peace was made between them, reluctantly on both sides, and the Fianna were able to turn to the problem of Fionn's enchantment.

Fionn told Kylta that it was the daughter of Culand the smith who had put the spell on him. He told him how she had lured him into the lake to search for the ring, and how he had come out of the water a broken man. It seemed that the only thing to do was to find her and get her to remove the spell. They cut some slender poles and made a litter to carry their frail king; then they picked him up on their shoulders and climbed slowly up to the fairy palace of Slieve Cullinn, where they believed that Milucra lived, deep underneath the ground with the Dé Danann. They set Fionn down gently and began to dig, determined to find her. They dug for three days and three nights and didn't stop for a single moment until they reached the cave where she lived.

Milucra, who had been listening to the sounds of digging getting nearer and nearer, was very much afraid when she finally faced the angry Fianna. She came and stood before them with the means to cure the enchantment held in her hand in a red-gold drinking horn. But she wasn't without spirit. She hesitated for a while: in spite of the fierce men she was reluctant to give up her hold on the king.

And then she saw Oscar and all thoughts of marrying Fionn left her. Oscar was young and handsome and manly and she fell in love with him on the spot. Without a word and without letting her eyes leave Oscar's face, Milucra handed the drinking horn to Fionn.

The trembling old man lifted it and drank – and immediately returned to his own shape. He stood, strong and handsome and once again Fionn Mac Cumhaill, leader of the Fianna, changed only in one respect: his hair was no longer gold, it was silvery grey.

The Fianna, relieved and happy to see him his own man again, crowded round to admire him, and all said that they liked the soft silver locks.

'I can restore your hair too,' Milucra said, still looking at Oscar, but Fionn was quite content. His men liked it and so did he; he chose to remain grey for the rest of his life.

Fionn passed the horn to Mac Reithe, who drank from it and then gave it to Diorraing, but when Diorraing drank from it it twisted in his hand and fell to the ground where it was immediately swallowed up. They all ran and tried to recover it – they knew that those who drank from it would be able to see the future – but dig and search as they could the horn was gone forever.

On the spot where it fell, a graceful narrow bush grew up and it still retains some of the gifts of the golden drinking horn: a reminder of the heroic days when the Fianna rode the length and breadth of Ireland. The bush has no name, nor can it be described, but those who look at it in the morning, having fasted from the previous night, will know at once all the events of the day to come.